ALSO BY ANDRE NORTON AND PHYLLIS MILLER

Seven Spells to Sunday

SOME OTHER BOOKS BY ANDRE NORTON

The Crystal Gryphon

Gates to Tomorrow:
AN INTRODUCTION TO SCIENCE FICTION,
edited by Ernestine Donaldy

Here Abide Monsters

The Jargoon Pard

No Night Without Stars

Quag Keep

Wraiths of Time

'Ware Hawk

Gryphon in Glory

(*Margaret K. McElderry Books*)

House
OF
Shadows

HOUSE OF SHADOWS

Andre Norton
and
Phyllis Miller

A Margaret K. McElderry Book

ATHENEUM   **1984**   NEW YORK

LIBRARY OF CONGRESS CATALOGING IN PUBLICATION DATA

Norton, Andre.
House of shadows.

"A Margaret K. McElderry Book."
Summary: Mike and Susan feel a mounting sense of
urgency and terror as they try to protect their younger
brother who seems threatened by an invisible and power-
ful force in a house that has long been in their family,
on which there is supposedly a curse.
[1. Ghosts—Fiction. 2. Dwellings—Fiction.
3. Family life—Fiction] I. Miller, Phyllis. II. Title.
PZ7.N82Ho 1984   [Fic]   83-16197
ISBN 0-689-50298-2

For Jenna, Julia and Janet

House of
Shadows

Chapter

1

" **D**IGBY'S GOTTA HAVE MORE ROOM! You're kicking him on purpose!" Tucker rammed a bony elbow into Susan's ribs. He knew just how to make it hurt.

There was no room to get away. Her head ached and her stomach had felt queer ever since they had had hamburgers and she had said "Everything," which meant gobs of mayonnaise, onion rings, dill pickle and—No! She tried not to remember and wished she could get the lingering taste out of her mouth.

"Shut up!" Mike ordered—in a low and determined whisper. "Stop being silly, Tuck. You know Susan can't kick an imaginary dog."

"Digby isn't 'maginary'!" Tucker's voice grew louder. "You said—all of you—I'd get Digby for my birthday. And my birthday was Wednesday—so there! Digby's here and Susan's got to remember that." He turned

3

his head to scowl at his older sister, his elbow ready for another sharp jab.

Susan scowled back. Tucker's imagination was sometimes just a little too much for anyone, even Dad or Mother, to handle. Because he had been promised a puppy—before they knew that they had to move—to Tucker the puppy was here, and it might be so for weeks. She swallowed a sigh and tried not to think of living with an invisible Digby.

Just now she only wanted to get out of this car, away from Tucker, from all the family. Mostly away from the unhappiness that rode with all of them for what seemed endless miles and miles—slept with them overnight in the motels and made lumps in her throat past which it was so hard to push food.

"You keep quiet back there. Your mother has a headache!" Dad's voice, cracking through the air, had all the sharpness it had carried for days now. Sometimes that even made Tucker listen. Now it hurt Susan's ears. She clapped both her hands tightly over her stomach and shut her eyes. She—she was going to be sick again! That was the worst misery of all.

"Susan's sick!" Trust Tucker to read the signs and give her away. "Better stop—she looks bad. She might throw up all over Digby."

Mother's head turned slowly. There was a frown of pain between her eyes, and Susan, who had tried to wither Tucker with a look, saw it. One of mother's bad headaches! If they were home she could lie down and use an ice pack to make her feel better. Susan gulped. This was maybe *her* fault—part of it anyway. She had

4

been carsick twice and . . . She clapped both hands to her mouth hastily as the car slowed, drawing to the side of the interstate highway.

Mother jerked open the door and Susan somehow got out. Mostly fell, she thought, as her knees hit hard into gravel. She lost the hamburger and a lot more, her misery of body for a minute driving out the other misery in her mind. Mother did not hold her head this time. Dad, muttering under his breath, came with a roll of paper towels in one hand.

Susan was limp with misery as she took a handful of ruffled up paper to wipe her sweating face.

"Better?" Dad did not sound quite so sharp now.

Susan drew a deep breath and nodded. "All right now," she said, holding Dad's hand as he pulled her up, leaning against him until she was sure that her feet and legs were going to work properly.

"How about you, Pat?" Dad lifted Susan into the station wagon, but he was watching Mother who had both hands to her face, covering her eyes, her head resting against the high part of the car seat.

"I'll do," she answered. Her voice sounded as if it came from a long distance away.

Dad got into the car and pulled out the map stuck in one of the sun visors, shaking it out wide.

"What was that last sign, Mike?"

"Funny word—something like Onadilla . . ."

"Hmm—" Dad ran his finger along the map. "All right, we're nearly there then. Just hold on, Pat."

He was watching Mother very closely as he folded the map. Susan, weak and shaken, knew that he was

5

worried. She wondered if anything was ever going to be comfortable again. Right now she did not see how it could be.

This had all started back home in Florida, at the Cape, about two months ago. It seemed such a long, long time since the day Dad came home with bad news. The space mission had been washed out because the government did not have any money to try more experiments. All Dad's department had been given what Mike called "pink slips," though Susan had never seen Dad holding one. What it did mean was that they must change their whole way of life and things would be a lot harder. Susan quickly learned not to ask questions. Mother simply kept telling her that nothing could be decided yet.

The whole last part of the summer had been spoiled. There were no trips to Seaworld or Disney. Then Francie and Karin went to visit their aunt in Carolina and Susan did not even have anyone to go around with. Mike would not talk most of the time—stayed in his room and read or said he was reading. Mike wanted to be a space pilot and thought about nothing else. But if there were not going to be any more missions—then how could he?

Tucker was the one who did not worry. All he thought about for weeks (and talked about until they were nearly crazy) was the puppy he had been promised for his sixth birthday. He had really blown up when Dad told him at last there was not going to be any puppy, because they were moving—North where there was no place for a dog.

They were going to stay with Great-Aunt Hen-

6

drika—a person who had never been more than a name at the bottom of a birthday or Christmas card as far as Susan knew. Of course, the cards had always included a crisp five dollar bill, and at Christmas there had come a big fancy box of cookies and candy. But she was not real as far as the three younger Whelans were concerned. The main point was that they—she, Mike, and Tucker—were going to live with Great-Aunt Hendrika in some kind of a funny old house way up in New York State for nobody knew how long.

Dad and Mother (and this was the strangest of all) were going back to school. At least Mom was. Dad was going to teach and write a book. But Mother wanted her degree so she could get a special job. They were NOT going to stay at Great-Aunt Hendrika's, but were going on to a college where they would live until they could make what Mother and Dad kept saying were "other arrangements."

The only thing Susan knew about Great-Aunt Hendrika, beside the fact that she had offered them a place to stay, was that she had cats. She had said that in her letter and that her cats did not like dogs. So there was no puppy. Except that Tucker, as usual, refused to accept what he did not like—and so Digby came along. But cats could not dislike an invisible puppy, so that ought to be all right.

Susan closed her eyes and tried to forget her uneasy stomach. If they could only *get* there—so she could be by herself where it was quiet and she did not have to listen to Tucker, did not even have to think or worry for a while—that was all she wanted.

Mike hardly spoke at all. The first day they had

started packing, he had gone out with a big box into which he had crowded all his space models—and he had come back empty-handed. Mike was not someone you could ask questions, so Susan was left to wonder what had become of the collection he had made so carefully and hung up in his room. Maybe he had given them away. All he had packed to send with their belongings were his books.

She wondered what kind of a school they would be going to this fall. Great-Aunt Hendrika lived in a small town, that much Dad had said. What kind of schools did they have in New York State? Would there be some girls like Francie and Karin? No—she did not want to know new people. It was always hard for Susan to meet strangers. Maybe the space program would start again and they could all go home. Things did happen like that sometimes—good things.

They turned off the interstate into a side road, and, when that curled around, they turned again. There were bushes growing around old, tumbled-down stone walls, and Susan caught sight of a dak metal sign with walls, and Susan caught sight of a dark metal sign with raised lettering, firmly fixed to a rock nearly as tall as the station wagon. But they swept past before she could read any of the words on it.

"Candiaga," Dad spoke for the first time since they had left the interstate.

The car came down a dip in the road and there were houses at last. Most of them were set well back and had fences or walls between them and the road. The car traveled along a brick-paved street now. The houses and buildings were partly hidden by a lot of trees and

8

more bushes. Some people working in their yards looked up as the station wagon went by. Everyone had sweaters on—it was a lot cooler here.

Dad slowed down to turn away from some stores and a gas station. This street was even narrower. Then it seemed they were heading out into the country again as the wall of a cemetery slid by. One more turn—this time through an opening in a fence which was painted white. The tires of the car crunched on gravel as Dad slowed to a stop before a house.

Susan sat and stared at the queerest house she had ever seen. It looked—weird. That was the only word for it—a favorite of Francie's—simply weird.

The main part was stone and was two stories high, fronted by a long porch that ran the full length of the building. To the right stood a tower, like a piece from a castle that had been stuck on here in an absent-minded way. Because it certainly did not seem a proper part of the rest of the house at all.

The edge of the porch roof was trimmed with what looked like wooden lace, and there was lattice work at either end up which grew vines. Around the windows Susan could see pointed casings with bits of trimming too.

Curtains were pulled firmly over the windows so no one could see inside the house; it did not want people. That thought came into Susan's head in a queer way. It was as if the house had locked its own doors and windows so that no one could come inside.

Tucker flopped across Mike to stare out. Now he said firmly: "I want to go home. Digby don't like this house. We want to go *home!*"

Mike clapped one hand over his brother's mouth, held him when Tucker started to fight. Leaning down, the older boy repeated his earlier order: "Shut up!"

Susan swallowed twice. For once she agreed entirely with Tucker, something which very seldom happened. She did not like this house either. And she wanted nothing more than to start driving back to their own home—their real home.

The wide door under the shadow of the porch roof opened and a woman came out. She was as tall as Dad and wore dark brown slacks and a sweater of the same color, with a green shirt collar showing above the sweater.

Certainly she was not Susan's idea of a great aunt. Maybe she was someone else who lived with Great-Aunt Hendrika, because her hair wasn't even gray. It was black, and she did not have an old lady's face. There was no softness about the chin, nor were there even many wrinkles. She walked fast, as if she knew just where she was going and why. Now she held out a hand to shake Dad's as he climbed out to meet her.

There was no kissing—even though this turned out to be Great-Aunt Hendrika after all. She shook hands with them instead—even with Tucker, who appeared so subdued by her briskness that he extended a sticky paw. And she spoke as quickly and emphatically as she walked. The Whelans were simply taken over, marched inside, parceled out among some bedrooms, before Susan really understood what was going on.

"She's like Commander Harris." Mike ventured on a single sentence as he trudged upstairs, lugging two canvas carryalls, Susan bumping behind him with an-

10

other, as well as a plastic bag filled with to-be-washed laundry.

Mike was right—Great-Aunt Hendrika was exactly like the commander, and they were soldiers being marched around. Moments later Susan stood in the middle of the room into which she had been directed and looked about her, bewildered, unhappy, feeling the misery rising inside again.

This was not in the least like her room at home. There was a wooden bed with very high ends—dark and carved. Across it, instead of her cheerful Holly Hobby spread, was a cover of dull, faded-looking blue. There were strips of rag carpet crossing bare flooring— one by the bed, one before a bureau that had a marble top and a mirror so high it nearly touched the ceiling. Was Great-Aunt Hendrika poor even though she lived in this great big house? All these ugly old pieces of furniture and just those two little pieces of woven rags for the floor—that looked poor to Susan.

The walls were covered with paper on which were big flowers. They were faded-looking, too—blue blossoms with tangled vines holding them up. There were four pictures, one exactly in the center of each wall. One was of a basket with a big blue bow on its handle and a fat, white, long-furred kitten lying in it. Another was of little girls wearing long dresses, dancing around in a circle. The other two—one between the windows and one by the bureau were too dim for her to see from where she stood.

To one side of the bed was another piece of furniture with a marble top and a lamp on it. There was also something else. Four books were set up stiffly between two polished stones that kept them from falling over.

In another corner was a fourth piece of furniture, a big cupboard which was not built in as a real cupboard ought to be—but which stood by itself. She studied its double doors unhappily—it looked like the sort of place in which something might hide.

Susan kicked aside the bag of laundry and made herself go over and pull open the cupboard door. Of course it was empty. There was only a rod across with hangers on it. She opened the other side to find shelves and a couple of drawers. Her nose wrinkled.

There was a queer smell. Was it bug spray, the kind they had used at home? No, this smelled more like Mother's bath powder—sharp but rather nice. Susan ran a hand along one of the shelves and brushed against a dried-up stem that still had bits of purplish flowers sticking to it. The smell came from that. But who would want to put dead flowers in a cupboard?

"Sue . . ."

Tucker had edged around the door from the hall. His face was still dirty. He had twisted sticky hands in the front of his T-shirt until it was what Mother called a disgrace. Now he came over to catch at Susan's sleeve.

"Sue, do we have to stay here?" There was such urgency in his voice that she was surprised. Tucker's normal reactions to things he did not like could be and usually were very loud and clear. Now he spoke almost in a whisper and kept looking around, as if he thought someone might be listening—someone he did not want to notice him.

"Yes—for a while."

12

Tucker ran his tongue across his lips. He had not loosened his hold on Susan.

"I don't like it here. It—it's scary!"

"It's just old. I guess Great-Aunt Hendrika's too poor or something to fix it up right." Susan kicked at the edge of the nearest rag runner.

"I—" For the first time Susan could remember Tucker seemed to have lost his voice. Then he jerked at her arm. "You come—please, Sue!"

Tucker certainly was changed. What in the world had happened to him? Susan was so amazed she actually allowed herself to be drawn across the hall— to the room to which Tucker had been assigned.

It was like hers and yet there was a difference. The bed did not have a high head and foot, but four stubby posts instead, and it was lower to the floor. There was a bureau and another large, dark cupboard. But there was also a small table near the window and a wooden chair of a size to fit Tucker. The paper on the walls could not be seen except in small patches for it had been pasted over with all kinds of cut-out pictures, bewildering to look at because there were so many of them—all colors, sizes and shapes, and all old. Some were yellowish and so faded you could hardly make them out.

In the middle of the table stood a train. It was old, too, made of wood not metal. The cars were hardly more than solid blocks mounted on small bent wheels; the engine had only part of a smokestack. It was like a train Susan had seen pictured in a history book.

Tucker simply stood in the middle of the room, no longer looking at Susan, but turning his head slowly

13

while he viewed the mass of pictures on the wall.

"Well!" They both jumped at the sound of Mike's voice, which appeared to come out of the air. A moment later he was with them.

"Comic books yet!" He waved at the picture-covered walls. "Somebody sure spent a lot of time in here, didn't they?"

"But it's all old—it couldn't have been Great-Aunt Hendrika." Susan had had a wild idea, for only a moment or two, that all this had been done to amuse Tucker. But it could not be true—these were old, old pictures.

"No," Mike answered. "This is a real old house, the family has owned it for a long time."

"How long?" Tucker wiped his hand across his mouth again, appearing more his usual bouncy self.

"About two hundred years." Mike said.

"There isn't anything *that* old!" Tucker *was* his usual self.

"Up North here there is. This house was built before the Revolutionary War—when all this country was just a wilderness full of Indians—"

"Then why did anyone want to come way out here and build a house?" Susan asked.

"I don't know. Dad talked about it once when he got some papers to sign."

"But it looks so queer. Did they use that tower for a lookout place when there were Indians?" For the first time Susan could see a reason for the odd shape of the house.

"No. The tower and all the part behind it must have been added later. People living here might have built

14

on bits from time to time."

"Like Francie's swimming pool." Susan thought of the only thing she had ever seen added to an already-built house.

"No swimming pools here," Mike said. "But there could have been families with more children. Then they would have built more rooms. This must have been a child's room for a long time. Mine's different."

Tucker was already at the door. "Digby and I want to see. Come on, Mike, show us."

They went down a short space of hall, but not through the door Mike had left open—for a very good reason. The space there was well occupied. Green eyes surveyed them with a vast lack of interest. Those eyes were set in a wide black furred head, part of which now split in a yawn, to display very pointed white teeth.

This was the largest cat Susan had ever seen. He must weigh pounds and pounds. Now he rose and stretched his forefeet well out before turning his head toward the room he had guarded and uttering a very odd sound, which was more squeak than a mew.

From the room came a second cat. This one was long and slim, smaller than the black. The eyes in a dark brown Siamese mask were brilliantly blue and just as cool when turned on the children.

"Sic 'em, Digby!" Tucker pushed past Susan. "Go and get 'em, boy!"

Perhaps being invisible also made Digby cautious. He certainly did not reveal his presence. The cats eyed the Whelans for another long, blinkless moment, then turned to pace in a dignified way toward the stairs.

Tucker snorted. "They're afraid," he said defiantly. "Those old cats. They knew Digby would chew 'em right up. So he will if he sees them coming back. What was that one doing in your room, Mike? You don't want any old cat hanging around here!"

Mike pushed wide the door and they entered a room not unlike Susan's. Except the pictures on the wall did not display a half-sleepy kitten or girls dancing. Instead there was one over the bed showing a river with a paddle-wheeled steamboat plowing through the water, while two of the others were of soldiers. One showed a troop wearing three-cornered hats, led by a mounted officer on a white horse. The other was of a building with thick walls from which protruded the mouths of cannons—woolly smoke half hiding some of them. On the ground below, men with long-barreled guns advanced at the urging of several sword-waving officers.

"More history." Mike waved at the pictures. "I guess we are not going to get away from it here."

"What's that?" Tucker pointed to an object hung by itself, though it was certainly not a picture. It looked like a curved horn held up by dusty colored straps as thin as shoelaces.

"A powder horn."

"Powder horn?" Tucker was completely at a loss. "What kind of powder and why did they keep it in a horn? And why is it here?"

"Powder for the old guns," Mike told him. "They didn't have bullets like we do now. They had to pour powder down into the gun before it would fire. That's the kind they used when they fought Indians. I guess

16

they did it right around here."

To Susan's surprise Tucker was backing slowly away, his eyes on that hanging horn. There was an odd look on his face. Tucker . . . why . . . Tucker looked frightened!

"I want to go home—this is a—I want to go home!" His voice scaled up. Susan braced herself. Tucker was about to have one of his screaming fits.

"Tucker!"

Dad came into the room and his hands closed on Tucker's slightly hunched shoulders. "You need cleaning up. Then we are going to have supper. And you are to be quiet. Mother's gotten asleep and she's not to be awakened."

There *were* times when Tucker could be stopped. Susan drew a deep sigh of relief. This must be one of them. He had shut his mouth, and he had not struggled when Dad took him out.

Mike shrugged as he glanced again at the powder horn. "Wonder what it was like living back then?"

Again Susan was surprised. Mike lived mostly in the future. This was the first time she had ever heard him wonder about the past.

Chapter

2

SUSAN STRETCHED OUT IN THE BED, her eyes firmly closed. As long as she did so she could believe she was back in her own room. Only she ached all over from holding so still . . . and listening . . . It was the listening that was the worst. Because there were sounds she could not identify. Creaks—and once a rushing rattle, as if something were running right over the ceiling above her, so that she gasped, and her heart beat so fast she felt very strange.

She could not stay here, she could not! When Mother and Dad left tomorrow she would ask to go, too. Surely they could all live in a motel—or somewhere. They must!

Her eyes, squinted so tightly shut, began to hurt. At last she opened them slowly. There was a patch of moonlight on the wall. It spread across that silly kitten in its basket. Susan sat up in bed to deliberately stick out her tongue at the kitten.

She was not afraid—she was not! Only, though she had been so tired when she trailed upstairs that she thought she'd go right to sleep, the minute she crawled into this bed she was wide awake as if it were morning, time to get up again.

Old houses—this ugly old house—that was the trouble. Firmly Susan plumped herself down on her pillows. Dad and Mother would not make them stay here, though the way Great-Aunt Hendrika talked she had everything all settled. Just as if none of the Whelans had anything to say about what they were going to do. Great-Aunt Hendrika was certainly used to running things.

All that talk at supper about history—how this house was the oldest one in the valley. That it had been built by some great-great-great who married an Indian princess—or at least a chief's daughter. And that the land on which it stood was hers and the house too. Then came a war—that was the Revolution—and there had been a lot of trouble here—a big fight with the Indians. Great-Aunt Hendrika had given them a funny look, her lips tight together, when she discovered that none of them knew about the house and the people who had lived there—as if the Whelans were really stupid.

Susan pulled the sheet about her shoulders. Funny, all of a sudden it was cold. There was a blanket over the bottom of the bed, should she unfold that? But whoever had heard of sleeping under a blanket at the beginning of September? Maybe she should get up and close the window. However, somehow she would rather not get out of bed at all.

She shut her eyes, she was going to go to sleep and forget all about staying here. Perhaps you only needed to be firm (like Great-Aunt Hendrika) because Susan did go to sleep. Only to wake, to find herself sitting up in bed once more, her hands holding the sheet in a tight twist.

She had— No, it was gone. Though she strained to hear, there was no sound now. Nor could she remember her dream, just that it was a nasty one. She was so afraid that she tried to keep awake, but now she could not.

Something was watching her. Susan knew that before she opened her eyes. When she did, it was to see the Siamese cat seated at the foot of her bed, its tail tip curled neatly over its paws, its blue eyes fixed upon her. There was daylight—though it must be early. Perhaps it was all right to get up. She wanted to talk to Mike and see what he thought about asking Dad and Mother if they all could go along—not stay here.

Scrambling out of the wide bed Susan faced one of those other pictures on the wall. This did not look like a real picture and Susan's attention was caught enough to make her go closer and stand on tiptoe. It was a queer thing with trees and birds, an alphabet and numbers, one to zero. There was a cat and some birds which were too big for the trees among which they had been scattered. Right at the bottom, in what seemed much brighter colors—red and black mixed together— was a name, "Emily Kimble," and below that some numbers—all in black—"1840."

"Susan—" Mother stood in the doorway. She smiled

as she looked about. "My, what an exciting room, dear. This is a perfect period piece. I envy you—"

"Mother," Susan began uncertainly. What Mother was saying was something Susan could not understand at all. She knew Mother liked old things, that she used to keep magazines with pictures of old houses and the things in them. But how could anyone like this—this place? "Mother, can't we go, too—up to the college? We could stay at a motel . . . and . . ."

"Susan"—Mother's smile was not so wide now, that little line was coming back between her eyes—"I know that this is a big change for all of you. But it is a wonderful opportunity, too. You see Daddy's mother never cared much for family history, and Daddy was never here before. This is a chance for you to learn about your—let us say your roots. You remember the TV play we saw and you talked about in school? Everyone has roots, but many of us never have the chance to learn much about them. You will here. This house is nearly a museum—except it is not shut up away from people. The same family whose ancestors built it are still living here. And they are *using* old things—not just setting them away in cupboards and on shelves somewhere. Great-Aunt Hendrika writes books about history and the things that have happened in this region. She can tell you so much. And it is very, very good of her to ask you children to stay here until we can get settled.

"You know that we shall find a house when we can and then be together again. But for now Daddy and I will be in Utica and you here. We cannot afford to live in a motel—and besides you would find it very

21

dull. While to live here is going to be exciting."

Mother was talking faster and faster, as she sometimes did when she became nervous. Susan dared not even sigh. There was absolutely no hope of driving away today. She swallowed twice, and the cat yawned widely.

"This will be like a vacation—like Francie's in Carolina," Mother added. Then her voice became a little sharper. "Really, Susan, you must not bother your father, he has a hard time ahead. And we are very lucky, very, very lucky."

The lump in Susan's throat had swelled so large now that she could not even squeeze out words. She nodded as Mother went to look at that queer picture on the wall with its "Emily Kimble," as if that were suddenly very important.

"A needlework sampler, Susan—and so well preserved. Emily Kimble . . . 1840 . . . and look—" Mother tapped the glass over that queer mixture of trees, birds, alphabet and numbers with one forefinger. "Here is her age—eleven. Why, she was just as old as you when she sewed this, Susan. What beautiful work! I don't think anyone could do as well today, even if they were twice Emily's age."

"Why . . . " Susan tried wildly to find something to ask which would not bring back Mother's headache. "Why does it say 'Kimble'? I thought Great-Aunt's name was Kuydall, and you just said that the same family always lived here."

"Maybe Emily made this when she was a little girl and then married into the Kuydall family and brought

22

it with her," Mother suggested. "You can ask and find out—"

"Mommie!" That shriek could only come from one throat—Tucker's. And he was certainly well into one of his fierce times. Mother was through the doorway at once. Susan was still scrambling into her jeans so it was a minute before she could run barefooted after her.

"Mommie!" Tucker was standing in the middle of the room. He had pulled off the top of his pajamas and his face was red, his fists were waving in the air. In the middle of his bed sat the big black cat staring at him.

Before Mrs. Whelan could stop him, he hurled himself at the table to grab at the wooden train. It came apart as he snatched it up, leaving Tucker holding a single car, a solid block of wood. This he threw straight at the cat.

Susan could not see how he had missed. But, luckily, the block skimmed past the cat to thump into a pillow. With long practice Mother caught Tucker's shoulders and, though he wriggled and flailed out, she held on.

"Digby—"

To the complete surprise of both Susan and her mother the fight suddenly went out of Tucker. Instead he crumpled back against his mother, holding on to her now.

"Tucky . . . " Mother sat down on the edge of the bed, her arms around Tucker who was crying. Not as if he were angry, but rather as if he had been badly hurt. "Tucky, what in the world happened?"

Susan was crowded away from the door as Mike

came up behind her.

"He—Digby—the Indians—Digby's dead. He's all stiff with blood—and he's dead!" Tucker wailed. Susan shivered. He made it sound so real she half expected to see on the floor, or perhaps on the bed itself, the body of a small dog.

"Tucky, look at me!" Mother pried loose Tucker's tight hold, got her hand under his chin to force his head up. His eyes were squeezed tight shut, tears on his cheeks. "Tucky!" Mother's tone was even sharper. "Open your eyes!"

Again to Susan's wonder Tucker did as he was told. He stared up at Mother whose face was now close to his.

"Now, Tucky, where is Digby?" She spoke slowly, but with that tone that meant she would have an answer.

"He's dead—the Indian—he killed him! Right there!" Tucker pointed over Mother's shoulder. The large black cat stood up, paying no attention to the two who shared the bed with him, moved to one side, and jumped to the floor. But Tucker might not have seen that at all—he was still pointing to where the cat had been.

Mike twitched at the pillow Tucker had wadded up during his sleep and shook it. The wood train car Tucker had thrown rolled onto the floor.

"There's no Indian, Tucky. You had a bad dream. This stuff"—Mike waved a hand at the picture-covered wall—"is enough to make anyone dream. Digby's just asleep. Call him. Now!"

Tucker turned his head away. "He's all dead. The Indian hit him. Now he's gone and he'll never come back. He'll go with *them*—"

Susan was completely bewildered. "Who's them?" she asked. A dead invisible Digby and an Indian? Tucker's imagination was working overtime now.

Tucker smeared a hand across his face. "Just *them*," he said, and his mouth set. She knew the signs. Nobody was going to learn anything more from Tucker.

Now he pulled away from Mother, turned his back on her and the bed. For a wonder he was no longer red in the face and ready to roar.

"With them," he repeated. Then nodded his head vigorously up and down. "*They* want him and he likes *them*—he likes—Carl . . . "

Susan longed to ask, "Carl who?" Then she saw her mother making a sign with one hand. If Tucker's usual absorption in make-believe could be switched in another direction all the better. It would seem as far as Tucker was concerned the scene was now over. He padded across to pick up the plastic bag holding his toothbrush and washcloth as if moments earlier he had not been storming about.

Mike moved to the wall examining the pictures at about the height Tucker would easily view them.

"No Indians," he muttered. "Here's a couple of dogs—but there're certainly no Indians. Where did Tuck get that idea?"

Mother was pushing Tucker in front of her toward the bathroom down the hall, fresh clothes for him over her arm. She frowned at Mike in warning as they disappeared together.

Susan looked at the bed again. Tucky had made her almost see what he claimed was there—that nasty thing! She picked up the train car to set it back on the table.

"Mike, do you like this house?"

He shrugged. "It's a queer place. And it's sure a lot different from 1925 Palms Acre. But we're stuck with it, Susan. And we've got to keep our mouths shut. Dad and Mom have enough to worry about. We can stick it out for a while, anyhow."

He ran his hand along the pictured wall. "Wonder who stuck all this stuff up and why. Where did they ever get such a lot of pictures anyway? I suppose out of old magazines."

"Why did Tucky think up that awful thing about Digby? He never did anything like that before," Susan said.

Mike threw out his hands—just as Dad always did when he was faced with some question he could not answer. "Why does Tuck do anything? He sees an elephant in the backyard for a week—remember last summer?—and wants to get hay. Pulled up near all the grass to feed it, didn't he? Then there was that flying thing that lived in the garage. How long did that last? I'll admit he never killed one off before. They just disappeared when he thought up something new. We were talking Indians some yesterday. I think sometimes Tuck hears more and remembers part of it—the wrong way—than we give him credit for doing."

Susan sometimes tried to forget Tucky's imagination. It was very difficult to live with, though mostly it was just annoying, as Digby had been. Being told all the time that one was stepping on, or sitting upon, or not being pleasant to an invisible could be very tiring.

26

When Dr. Ramish had given Tucker those tests a couple of years ago he had said that he would eventually learn the difference between real things and what he imagined. All their friends back at the Cape had accepted Tucker's way of seeing things. Sometimes they even got interested enough to ask just what new invisible had moved in with the Whelans. Susan once had an idea Tucky could write books if someone would just put down what he said—he could be so *real* about it all. She had tried to keep a notebook about the thing in the garage. That had been really spooky, because Tucky had never come right out and described it—he just talked about it in a way that had made Susan rather glad she could *not* see it.

Still, never before had Tucker ever said one of his " 'maginaries," as he called them, was *dead*. She didn't like that.

She thought about Digby through breakfast, but forgot afterwards because Mother and Dad were leaving. They unpacked a lot from the back of the station wagon, leaving cartons and boxes on the front porch and in the downstairs hall. Then they drove off and Susan (though to think of riding at all made her stomach unhappy) wanted to be in the back seat.

Great-Aunt Hendrika, who had not been at breakfast, came out to say goodby. She had announced last night that her day was very different from that of other people, but she was used to it, and she intended to continue so. They did not have to suit their hours to hers, but she would expect them to keep to a schedule which she would discuss with them later. Both Dad and Mother had agreed readily for Mike, Susan and

27

Tucker—with a couple of very speaking looks, though such might be lost on Tucker.

Great-Aunt Hendrika and Tucker, Susan decided after she had watched the station wagon disappear, were somewhat alike. They both spoke as if they were right and what they expected of people was going to be done. Mother said Great-Aunt Hendrika wrote books—so perhaps she imagined just like Tucker, though Susan was sure she did not bring invisibles to live with her.

"Well now." Great-Aunt Hendrika broke into Susan's thought. Mike was pushing a couple of cartons around on the porch as if he thought he ought to do something with them, but did not know quite what. Mike often had fits of being helpful—but at intervals only. Tucker was squatting down at the edge of the gravel drive to look at a small plant.

"You've got a big green worm here," he announced.

"I am not at all surprised," Great-Aunt Hendrika answered. "There are brown, yellow, black and green worms—as well as a few of the ordinary red ones—always visiting—usually on plants I want most to have saved. Come on, Tucker, I have a few things to say, and I want open and listening ears.

"First, Mrs. Kingsley and her niece, Eloise Purdy, run this house. I may own it—they run it. They have their own rooms out in the carriage house, which was made into a cottage when I took over fifteen years ago. You are to listen to them when they want anything done to help in the house. I suppose you can make your own beds—Mike, Susan? There is the important matter of neatness—also some chores, about which Mrs.

Kingsley will tell you. Jim Baines runs the garden—if he needs help he'll tell you.

"I get up very early in the morning—I do not expect that from you. Also I retire at an early hour. My work hours are in the morning. I can only be interrupted for dire emergencies—none of which have ever arisen so far."

"What's a dire 'mergency'?" Tucker was paying attention, which was more than he did sometimes. Susan thought that Great-Aunt Hendrika had really gotten through to him.

"The house burning down, a tornado, or something of the sort." Great-Aunt Hendrika treated Tucker's comment with complete seriousness. "I work in the newer wing of the house—sleep there, too.

"School started last week, but since the length of your stay here is uncertain I have made arrangements as I do not believe in changing patterns too often. For twenty years I taught school." As if she did not see them, she suddenly glanced at the house. "It was only when I came here to live that, as you might say, I retired. My certificate is still in good order and I can set lessons that will pass muster for a while. Therefore"—she made a gesture at the door—"we shall see that you are not going to miss lessons and fall behind."

Mike straightened up from the cartons. The faint frown on his face had become a scowl. Susan guessed what was the matter. Mike wanted to be sure, very sure of good grades—he wanted to go to the Air Force Academy or maybe one of the universities where there were space studies. If you did not go to any regular school, how could you hope to make the right

29

grades for a scholarship? And he would *have* to have one now.

If he planned to offer any objections, he was not given a chance, for Tucker had moved up the single wide step to the porch to face Great-Aunt Hendrika, standing with his legs a little apart, his head back so he could look into her face. Great-Aunt was a tall person and her stiffness of back made her seem even taller.

"You look like her," he said as Great-Aunt paused for breath, "only she—" He shook his head, looking puzzled. "You don't have the funny thing she carried, the face with the crooked old mouth."

Susan took a small half-step forward. Tucker was at it again. Luckily he was not talking about Indians and a dead Digby. What was he going to bring into invisible life now?

"A face with a crooked mouth?" Great-Aunt Hendrika repeated slowly, staring down at Tucker, her face very stiff and odd-looking. "Now just where did you see that, young man?"

For the first time Tucker did not seem eager to share one of his flights of imagination. Instead he backed away a little, almost as if he were afraid. Then he shook his head violently.

"I—I'm not going to tell. It's a secret—a big secret!"

Great Aunt Hendrika's odd, stiff look did not disappear. Instead she spoke, not as if she were answering Tucker, but thinking aloud. "A big secret . . . yes, perhaps it is . . . or was. Now"—she blinked and was the same Commander-in-charge-of-the-troops she had been before Tucker had broken into her orders-of-the-day.

"It has become plainer through the recent years, I am sorry to say, that the art of reading, and that of writing, appear to be vanishing from the public schools. I have received a number of letters from time to time—from those old enough to know better—which are misspelled, ill-informed, and whose writers know nothing of simple rules of grammar—such as the proper sentence. The place to begin is the library. Shall we adjourn there?"

She was already at the door. Mike, still scowling, moved away from the cartons, while Susan grabbed at Tucker's hand. Tucker would have been in first grade this fall. He could not even read. If Great-Aunt Hendrika thought she could get Tucker to do anything he did not want to—well maybe they would see a fight as bad as if some Indians did come at them. Luckily, at this minute Tucker appeared willing to go along, not even dragging his already sticky hand out of Susan's hold.

They entered a square room on the same side of the center hall as the big dining room, but at the front of the house. One wall was broken by a fireplace so large that Susan thought all three of the Whelans could go and stand inside of it. On either side of that big black mouth were seats like park benches, only they had dark red cushions and high solid backs. There was a big desk at the far end of the room and a number of chairs scattered around, while the curtains at the long windows were also red and pulled back to let in as much light as possible. There were lamps here and there.

There were two tables—long narrow ones—topped by glass cases. They were display cases, with things lying inside to be seen, not touched.

However, the main part of the room was the books. Susan had never seen so many except in a public library. And even the library never showed on its shelves such old books with dusty-looking backs. Great-Aunt Hendrika waved one hand toward the nearest of the shelf-covered walls.

"The raw material of education," she said. "For a number of years this manor was a summer home only. And for most of those years one of the forms of entertainment was reading—to oneself or aloud for a family to enjoy. Books were bought and brought here for evenings, for rainy days, for information and pleasure. This section"—she stabbed one finger at some low shelves where there was a long row of big red books, looking all alike, with gold lettering on them, and some smaller ones—"belonged to the children. But you are free to go hunting in *any* section you want to. You don't know what you may be able to find. It may be quite surprising, even in this day and age." She was looking at Mike, who stood with his hands in his pockets carefully not looking, Susan was sure, at any shelf at all.

"I shall require regular hours to be spent here, making yourselves aware of what can be found by those willing to look." She turned to the big desk. "Over there you will find paper, pencils, and elbow room. You are to give me regular reports on your discoveries—for one week. At the end of that time I shall have finished my revision and be free. I shall also gain from your reports some idea of how we must then proceed."

Tucker pulled loose from Susan's hold. He might have been attentive to Great-Aunt Hendrika when they came in. Now he was again his own person and had gone to one of the glass-topped tables. Displaying his complete lack of attention, he demanded: "What are all those beads doing here?"

Susan expected Great-Aunt Hendrika to try to settle Tucker, as people usually did when he refused to pay attention. Instead she gave him an answer: "Those are to be read also, Tucker."

He stared at her as if startled that anyone might be able to match him in wild statements. "How do you read beads?" he asked.

For the first time Great-Aunt Hendrika displayed a small tight smile. "Suppose you learn, Tucker. An excellent way to begin. Who reads beads—and why? If you can answer that by the end of this week—well, I think that you will have made a quite acceptable beginning at expanding your education."

Chapter

3

As if great-aunt hendrika considered that she had fully explained
everything, she went swiftly out of the library, leaving
Tucker still staring after her. Susan and Mike moved
closer to the glass case to see what he had discovered.

There were different-colored beads there, right
enough, sewn into wide strips, making stiff patterns
with their colors.

"What did she mean really? You can't read beads!"
Susan asked Mike.

"Indian stuff," he answered.

Susan glanced hurriedly at Tucker—no more Indians, please! Luckily he had wandered away from the
case to make a slow exploration around the room, one
hand flipping along backs of old books.

"Tucker can't read . . ." Susan felt helpless. "He—if
she makes him stay in here he'll do something awful

and we won't be able to stop him."

"Then she'll learn." Mike did not appear to care. Nor did he, to Susan's surprise, seem to want to look at any of the books.

They were old and there was a funny smell in the room, as if the books were dead. She wrinkled her nose. She did want her question answered. How *did* one read beads? The answer must be here somewhere. She studied the wall cases. The filled shelves reached well above her head. Even standing on tiptoes she could not reach the top books. How did one go about finding things? She looked appealingly to Mike, who had gone to the nearest window and was staring out, his head turned firmly away and his shoulders set as stiff as Great-Aunt's.

Tucker completed his trip around the room and returned to hunker down before the section Great-Aunt had said contained children's reading. Now he asked: "Where's the TV? This is Saturday. It's time for *Space Raiders*—nearly."

Tucker might not yet wear a watch but, oddly enough, when he said it was time for this or that he was usually right.

"TV . . . maybe there isn't any—" Susan suddenly realized that there had been no set turned on to hear news last night, nor sound of any evening program.

"That's silly." Tucker got up to march determinedly toward the door. "Everybody's got a TV. I want to see *Space Raiders*!"

Susan trailed after him. To control Tucker was beyond her powers, but she still felt responsible for what he might do. He crossed the hall, pushed open the opposite door. They looked into another big room, but the corner of this one had been cut by part of the tower and that curved section was bright with sun. Shelves were in all the windows and held plants with flowers, or long, lacy ferns. A woman stood by the shelves using a watering pot, holding it in one hand while she picked off a yellowish leaf with the other.

"My, my, you're not doing too well," she said as Tucker and Susan reached the middle of the room. "A mite too much, or it is too little? We'll just have to wait and see. Now, look at calendula over here—see—that's the way to stand up."

Susan realized that the lady was talking to the plants, that she probably had not seen them yet. She was shorter than Great-Aunt Hendrika and her hair was not exactly white. It looked bluish. It was done up in waves and had a comb stuck in the back. Her face was round and she had a short nose turned up at the tip. She was dressed in a wide skirted dress with a ruffled hem, made of bright purple calico, and a ruffled blouse of white with purple flowers. Her glasses had very large lenses, which looked odd, as if her eyes should have matched by being twice as big as they really were.

"That's all," she was saying. "There will be a mite of plant food all around tomorrow. And mind you take in all the sun you can. Sun's what you need at this time of year—"

"You're talking to the plants," Tucker said.

The woman actually gave a little jump as she looked around.

"My goodness." She set down the watering pot. "You

36

certainly are Kuydalls—walk just like Indians. Or the way they always said Indians walked—so nobody could hear them."

"We're Whelans." Susan hastened to correct that. "I'm Susan and this is Tucker."

"And I am Mrs. Kingsley. There's another of you . . ." She looked inquiringly beyond Susan and Tucker.

"Yes, Mike."

"Why do you talk to them?" Tucker pointed to the plants.

"Because they're alive and they need to be noticed," Mrs. Kingsley answered. "How would you like it if day after day, when you were living right in the same house, no one ever spoke to you at all?"

Tucker looked from the plants to her and then back again. "Do they answer?" he asked with open interest.

"They do in their way—by growing stronger, blooming more. Where is that brother of yours? There is some settling in to be done. All those things in the hall and on the porch, we have to find places for them."

The children forgot the library as they carried some cartons up to their bedrooms and put others in an empty room farther down the same hall, which was for storage.

They did not have to do it all alone. Mrs. Kingsley produced a big apron, which covered most of her ruffly dress, and she called from the back of the house a girl who wore the same kind of dress—except hers was bright red, and her apron blue.

Mrs. Kingsley called her Eloise, but Eloise apparently had no wish to know the Whelans. She carried things upstairs as if she would rather throw them instead, stamping on every step, and she never spoke to the children. She was older, of course, she must be in high school, or maybe even going to college—and she looked cross whenever Susan happened to glance in her direction.

Mrs. Kingsley came tripping in as Susan brought up the last of the boxes in which her own things had been packed.

"It certainly needs neating up in here," she announced. "Now—" She opened the door of the big wardrobe to run her hand along the line of empty hangers. "If you do not have enough of these—tell me so. The drawers are ready, too." She went to the bureau pulling open one drawer after another. "Fold and put away. Your mother gave me the laundry bag. We will run the clothes through on Monday and hang them out—nothing like good clean air for drying. If you get right to work, Susan, you can put everything neat before lunch."

Such was the command in her voice that Susan was already unpacking before the door quite closed. She put effort into hanging up and smoothing out, too. Somehow she was very sure there would be an inspection of her efforts later and they had best meet with approval.

She was setting her school shoes straight in the bottom of the wardrobe and wondering if they were ever going to be school shoes again when Mike looked in.

"I'm to store the cartons in the storeroom," he told her and for the first time he grinned. "Great-Aunt's the Commander all right—but we've got the Sergeant on our tails as well." He stacked up the boxes Susan had emptied.

"Did you do your room?" she asked.

"Did it! That sourpuss of an Eloise looked at me and said she wasn't going—she had no time to wait on people. I can take a slight hint like that. What about Tucker?"

Susan sighed and got up from her knees. "I guess it's probably up to us. Nobody else will."

Mike nodded. "Nobody else better—not unless they want Tuck to explode. You know how he is."

Tucker was a very "that is mine, keep your hands off" person. Susan wondered dismally if they could even persuade him to let them deal with the muddle that must now be stacked in his room.

She stopped short in her surprise when she pulled open the door. There were cartons, yes, but they were empty and Tucker was just pushing shut the bottom drawer of the bureau.

"Tucky—"

He scowled at her. "I did it. It's all put away just like *she* said it had to be." He was between Susan and the now-shut drawer, and she knew better than to try to investigate just *how* things had been put away. "These empty ones"—he kicked at the nearest carton—"are to go back in that other room, she said that too." And, wonder of wonders, Tucker actually piled one on top of another, took a firm grip on what he held, and started for the door.

Susan scuttled out of his way. As he passed her he looked back over one shoulder:

"Did you hear 'bout us?"

"What about us?" Susan traveled along to ask, since Tucker showed no sign of halting.

"We're cursed—"

"We're what?" Mike demanded, as if completely shaken out of his own thoughts. "What do you mean?"

"That old Eloise—she said it. We're cursed." He disappeared into the storeroom with his load, leaving his brother and sister.

"She never talked to me at all," Susan said.

"I got about one sentence about not causing trouble," Mike returned. "What in the world did Tucker do this time?"

Though they cornered their brother and demanded to learn more, he only repeated that Eloise said they were cursed and that was that. Nor, he denied vigorously, had he done or said anything to make the sullen girl say such a thing.

Lunch was served in the old kitchen and Great-Aunt Hendrika did not appear. The room was large, with a fireplace so big Susan thought it might be a small room if someone wanted to add a door with a bit of wall on either side. There *was* a door—high up on one side— and when she dared to ask about that Mrs. Kingsley said it was the old oven, once used to do all the baking.

At one end of the room stood a very modern-looking stove, which she said Great-Aunt Hendrika had bought just two years ago. And there were walls of cupboards, as well as a big piece of furniture that looked like the dresser in Susan's room, but had shelves instead of a mirror on top. Those shelves were crowded with dishes. There was a bowl shaped like a head of cabbage, all green and shiny; a jug that was a cow, her mouth open for the milk to come pouring forth; plates with pictures on them. Too much to really see all at once—just like the pictures pasted up in Tucker's room.

"Where's the TV?" Tucker laid down half a peanut butter and jelly sandwich.

"TV?" To Susan's surprise Eloise, seated at the other end of the table as if to make sure of being as far from the newcomers as possible, answered. "There's no TV. Miss Kuydall don't allow one in the house."

Tucker actually looked shocked. "I want to see *Dr. Coffin*. He's on Saturdays—" His lower lip pushed out. "Everybody has a TV. There's got to be one!"

"Well, there isn't, not here." It was plain that being able to pass along that information pleased Eloise.

Susan prepared herself for an outbreak from Tucker. At the same time she thought regretfully of the afternoon movie.

Mike ate on silently. He had finished his sandwiches and was busy with a large section of pie. Mrs. Kingsley was drinking a second cup of coffee. She looked over it straight at Tucker.

"There's a job waiting, young man. Come next Friday we have to deliver jars to the church for the big canning bee. In case you don't know about such things, the farmers hereabouts donate extra fruit and garden truck to the Ladies' Aid, and we put them up for the winter. Good for church suppers and for any folk down on their luck. The church is glad to get all the extra jars they can, so this afternoon we'll cull them out down cellar."

Eloise slammed down her glass of cider. Coke was

41

something else not to be found in Great-Aunt Hendrika's house.

"It's—" she was beginning in a very angry voice when Mrs. Kingsley interrupted her.

"It's part of your job. You go up and change into jeans before you begin it, too. Lucky we've got us some helpers here.

"That fruit cellar hasn't had a good turn out in years. Like as not we're going to find some things back in corners that the Kimbles left. Good thing to get it done once and for all."

Susan dared to ask a question as she remembered the picture sampler on her bedroom wall.

"I thought the Kuydalls always lived here. Who were the Kimbles?"

Mrs. Kingsley paused. For a moment Susan thought there was an odd look on her face, almost as if she had said something she was sorry for.

"Kuydalls built the manor." She spoke sharply, scraping the plates as if she were annoyed. "But they didn't always live here. One of the Kuydall girls married a Kimble. Later the Kuydalls came back. They had lived in New York City for a long time—never were farmers—had something to do with a bank. They just visited here in summer."

Eloise stood up putting her own plates together with a clatter.

"And wished they hadn't," she said.

Mrs. Kingsley turned so quickly to face her niece that the ties of her big apron caught with a jerk on a drawer handle.

"That's enough of that, young lady!"

Eloise looked as if she wanted to answer back, then shrugged and walked out of the kitchen, her full skirt twitching like a cat's tail.

Cat. Susan was suddenly aware that the two cats were in the kitchen too. Having left polished plates, they had moved to sit in front of a door at the other end of the room, a door that was very solid-looking with large iron hinges.

Tucker, who had not carried on his demand for TV, slid off his chair and went to that door also. Now he looked around.

"Do we have to go down?"

"Down?" Susan was puzzled. Down where? What did Tucker mean—down? How could one go down—into the ground?

"Fruit closet's in the cellar, yes,"—Mrs. Kingsley was rinsing plates. "Not like the old days though. Miss Kuydall had new lighting put in just last year."

Cellar—Susan had heard of them, but she had never seen one back home. How had Tucker known about it?

He had backed away from the door, bumping into the big black cat that spit and struck out. Mrs. Kingsley shook her head at the cat.

"None of that, Josiah! They fancy going to the cellar —seems like they think they can hunt down there. We'll have to be sure we get them up again when we're through. Now"—she surveyed the children—"you all look as if what you have on will wash. This will be a good dusty job before we're done. As I said, a lot of the jars have been on the shelves a mighty long time.

43

From before Miss Kuydall came here, when old Mrs. Elsie was still alive. She believed in canning. Though why she put up so much when there were so few here to eat it, goodness only knows.

"Most of the jars of preserves must have gone to sugar long ago, and the vegetables might make a person sick they're so old. Jim will dump it all in the compost pit back by the shed and cover it up, come Monday. Have to wash out the jars after that."

She tied a towel over her waves of hair, then rolled up the sleeves of her dress. "Baskets down there waiting to be loaded." She threw open the door. The cats streaked past her. She reached inside to feel along the wall and pressed a button. What had been a dark and shadowy place was now lighted so she could lead the way down a flight of stone stairs guarded by wood railings.

There was a damp smell that Susan disliked. She did not want to help in this particular chore. Only Mike was right, Mrs. Kingsely was very much the Sergeant and they were a squad being pressed into service.

Mike came behind her, Tucker between them. Her smaller brother caught Susan's hand and squeezed it. There were lights enough. Also they could see slits of windows, very narrow and very high up, with bars across them. To one side were big stone tubs, and standing at the end of one, a thing Susan recognized, from a postcard Mother had once bought at a restored village museum, as a large pump.

Ahead was a hall with wooden walls, from which

whitewash flaked off. Mrs. Kingsley pulled open a door that scraped across the floor. Again she reached inside to turn on a light. They came to a windowless room which, like the library, was walled with shelves. Susan could not have believed there were so many glass jars and big crocks anywhere. All were arranged in neat rows—and some of those rows were double and triple, so that the outer jars perched on the very edge.

Mrs. Kingsley had brought several clean but ragged cloths and now she began to flick one across the front of the jars. Their labels were brownish and the markings on most of them were very faded so Mrs. Kingsley had to pick them up to read them.

"Baskets in the storage room across the hall," she said. "Get them, please."

Mike went first and then Susan, Tucker still holding her in a grip that really hurt now. She tried to pry her fingers loose, but he did not even look at her—just held on as if he could not let go even if he wanted to. The other room was dark, and Mike had trouble finding the light switch. Tucker gave a sudden jerk, dragging Susan back.

"No!"

His face was not flushed as it was when he was angry—rather he looked scared.

"Not in there!" Before Susan could find out what was the matter, he at last loosed his hold on her and was running, back to steps, out of the cellar. She did not try to follow him—though she would have liked to.

There was a chill down here, something like that chill she had felt in the middle of the night, and she shivered. The smell of dust or old stone and wood, or whatever it was, was strong. She tried not to breathe in too deeply.

Mike dragged at a pile of baskets—big ones like those in which oranges were shipped at Christmas time.

"Let the kid go," he said. "This—this is a place—" He paused as if he could not find the right words.

"I don't like it," Susan said, keeping her voice low. "Mike, I don't like this house. I don't want to stay here."

He shook his head. "We've got to—until Mom and Dad get settled. Don't give Tuck any ideas, he has enough of his own. Can you drag these over?"

Susan dragged, pulling a pile of baskets back to where Mrs. Kingsley was talking to herself. Or rather she was reading aloud the labels of jars, pushing some jars to one side and some to another:

"Plum, 1970—Cherry, 1969—Peach, 1950—Elderberry and apple, 1940. 1940! Just load these in, child. And all those crocks. Those must have been pickles. I wonder what's in them now—would rather not know. Jim will have a fine mess dealing with these."

They did not have to carry any filled baskets up through the house Susan discovered. There was a side opening into the cellar—big flaps of door that folded back—so it was easier, two of them to a basket, to lug them up that way. Mrs. Kingsley was finding more and more containers over which she shook her head. Eloise had appeared and was helping to carry, but Susan began to wonder if they would have to clear out everything. When at last, blackened with dust and with aching backs, they brought out the last basket, Mrs. Kingsley declared that the fruit cellar was now in passable order.

Susan and Mike were dismissed to clean themselves up. Mrs. Kingsley had not seemed to notice that Tucker was not with them. However, during all that time of packing, pulling, and lifting, Susan's mind was not at ease over what the youngest Whelan might be doing. She suspected that Mike had the same worry from comments he made when he paused to rest.

Tucker was not in his room where Susan looked at once when she went upstairs. She passed the news to Mike at the door of the bathroom as she ducked in to wash. Sometimes Mike had a better chance of handling Tucker, and she was so tired that even her fear of what her brother might be doing did not matter so much.

It was not until she found Mike missing too that she hurried downstairs. The library door was open just a little and she heard voices. At least they did not sound as if there was a fight going on and she ducked in quickly.

Tucker was there all right, sitting on the floor by those children's books. But the one he had spread out flat on the faded red and gold of the carpet was a much larger one than any she remembered having seen, even on the bottom shelves among the tall books.

"There is the face—" Tucker stabbed the right-hand page with a fingertip. "She had it. I saw it. Only *she* looked all different. But the face—it is just like the one!"

Susan moved up behind the boys. Mike was kneeling

beside Tucker, leaning over the book, but Susan could see a colored picture on the page Tucker pointed to. The colors were not bright—rather pale, in fact, as if they had been put on the paper a long time ago. There was no printing, only writing. That was also very faded, brown instead of black.

The face Tucker had discovered was not a pleasant one. Nor was it a real face. It looked as if it had been carved out of wood, with feathers stuck on top of the head instead of hair. There was hair too—coarse and strange, caught up in a knob above the forehead. The eyes were big and outlined with white, then red, and there were black lines down the cheeks with some dots on the chin. The mouth was lopsided—dropping farther down on one side than the other. As for the rest, the color of the face was a dull brown like garden earth.

Susan did not like the look of it at all. "What is it?" she asked.

"False Face," Mike said. "A secret society of the Mohawks—old Indian stuff."

Tucker slapped his hand palm down on the painting. "She had it . . . and . . ." He pushed back from the book. "I don't want to see it—take it away!"

"Where did you find it?" Mike closed the book, but still held it.

Tucker shook his head. "I looked—I knew—and I looked." Then he shut his mouth firmly.

Mike juggled the book across his knee. "Maybe you found more than you know, Tuck," he said slowly. "I want a better look at this."

He got up and laid the big book on the desk.

"What is it?" Susan asked for the second time.

"Sort of a diary, I think. Somebody who lived here and knew about Indians." He grinned. "Maybe just the sort of thing the G.-A.—the Great-Aunt—wants us to hunt for. If it is, we can surprise her with how quickly we've caught on."

Tucker shook his head. "I don't want to see that again!" he stated with all his old firmness.

Chapter
4

GREAT-AUNT HENDRIKA DID APPEAR for breakfast the next morning. They ate, not in the kitchen, but in the dining room which, in spite of sun outside, seemed dark in corners where pieces of heavy old furniture crouched. As she added a half-spoonful of jam to toast she studied the Whelans critically.

Susan suddenly remembered that she had given her hair only a quick comb through. She had been too busy making sure that Tucker had a clean face and hands— it being her day to do that. She and Mike, as Mother had them promise before she left, were to divide that duty between them.

"Church at ten—Mr. Reever's second Sunday," Great-Aunt Hendrika announced. "A dress, not jeans, Susan—and proper shirts . . . " Now she looked at Mike.

"Tucker . . . " Susan began. She could not think of

Tucker sitting through a church service speechless and quiet. He went to Sunday school at home, but that was different because he was in the class Mother taught so he usually behaved.

"Short service." Great-Aunt Hendrika reached for her coffee cup. "No reason why a boy his age can't stay through it. How did you come out in the library yesterday?"

"We were helping Mrs. Kingsley—in the cellar mostly," Mike answered for them all. "There were a lot of jars of old preserves she wanted taken out to be dumped. Then we had unpacking—"

Great-Aunt Hendrika set down her coffee cup with a thump. "The church canning bee! Martha . . . " Mrs. Kingsley had just come in from the kitchen. "I'd forgotten about it."

"Well, Miss Hendrika, those old jars should have been cleared out long ago. Things there for nearly thirty years, some of 'em. We stacked them all outside and Jim can see to the dumping. Take a lot of washing up though—and there are stoneware crocks—those we'd better keep."

Great-Aunt Hendrika settled back a little in her chair. "You give me an idea, Martha. Those crocks ought to have some value. They are Early American, and that's what people are looking for. We'll certainly never use them all."

Mrs. Kingsley nodded as she sat down and pulled the napkin off the basket she had carried in. It was full of blueberry muffins, which she offered first to Mike. "You mean you could put 'em in the sale of your cousin's things, Miss Hendrika. Yes, you could. I'll just pass a word to Sam about it this morning. After all it is an auction of Kimble-Kuydall things."

Great-Aunt Hendrika turned her coffee cup around and around on its saucer, staring down at it in an odd way as if she did not really see it at all.

"I always thought Hester would change her mind. Seemed unfair she would never come here to call, nor take much of what Aunt Elsie left. Goodness knows, I talked to her enough about it. Until she really put me off that one time." Now she looked cross.

"I think she always remembered Grover. She took it hard when he died."

"Yes, and I wasn't here." Great-Aunt Hendrika straightened up stiffly again. "I had no choice in that matter. Jobs were hard to get and I could not take time off just two months after I was hired."

"Now, she never held that against you, you know that, Miss Hendrika. It was just that she had to handle things, and it got too much for her with Mrs. Elsie taking on the way she did and all. It was really hard on the old lady. Her remembering so well about Richard, Tod, and James. Her mother never forgot and was always talking about them right up to her dying day. I remember *my* mother saying that. She was just a little girl herself but everyone talked—"

"They always do!" Great-Aunt Hendrika's voice was very sharp. Mrs. Kingsley's face got pink, and she was suddenly busy with her bacon and scrambled eggs.

Eloise had not come to breakfast. She had gone into town the evening before and was staying over at a friend's house. But the cats were present, sitting together, each with a plate before it. Great-Aunt Hendrika pushed her chair back a little and took a dish with scraps of egg and some bits of buttered toast on it, stooping to divide that into equal portions. "Manners, Josiah—Erasmus . . . "

They waited with dignity until she was through, and then sampled what she offered. Great-Aunt Hendrika continued to watch them eat.

"Sunday morning treat," she said as if explaining, though she did not look around at the Whelans. "Now" —she did glance across the table—"if you are finished . . . " She looked down at the watch on her wrist. "We have time for some.talk. I had a good day yesterday—got through more of my revision than I had hoped. So you did not get to the library? No matter." She nodded. "You have an hour or so to look around this morning. Let's see what can be done."

They trailed behind her into that darkish room. Great-Aunt Hendrika threw a light switch, and this time there was a chance to see the rows of books better. She stopped before the section she had shown them the day before and pointed to the row of red and gold books.

"*St. Nicholas* Magazine—bound. That was a real treat. Dip into it and see for yourself. Do you know"— she stood with her head a little on one side—"this collection could represent a history of sorts in itself—what the children of this country read for over a hundred years. *What Katy Did.*" She pulled out a book with a worn cover, then shoved it back again. "*Granny's Wonderful Chair.*" That looked even duller on the outside, but she flipped it open and peered at the flyleaf. "To Emily from Papa, Christmas 1869.

"Henty, now—I remember when Orrin started on Henty. *Under Drake's Flag. By Pyke and Dike.* Coffin— *The Boys of '76* . . . And here's *Hildegarde* and *Margaret Montford* and *The Peterkin Papers* . . . " Her voice sounded excited. "We always were book people and somehow the favorites ended up here, brought along when the Washington Square house was finally closed."

"Please . . ." Now that Great-Aunt Hendrika had paused Susan dared to explain what she had not had a chance to do earlier. "Tucker can't read. He's just been to kindergarten—"

"Any child," Great-Aunt Hendrika announced firmly, "can read if made interested enough, and he has normal intelligence. I am sure that Tucker has that." She looked to where he was standing eyeing the shelves with none of his usual frowns, but rather as if he expected something interesting to happen.

"What do you want to read about, Tucker?" Great-Aunt Hendrika asked.

"Indians," he answered without any hesitation. "Indians—the ones who were here." He jabbed one finger into the air as if pointing to someone really present.

Invisible Indians! Susan swallowed nervously. Oh, please not any more invisible Indians!

Great-Aunt Hendrika nodded. "Good enough!" She hunted along the shelves before her and pulled out two books. One was larger and, though its spine, which had faced the room, was dull and faded, there was a bright picture of an Indian on the cover. The other, smaller book had the picture of a boy and girl stamped on the binding.

Susan could read the title of that: *The Indian Twins*.

"Now see what you can make out of these—No"—she shook her head at Susan—"let him make discoveries for himself. I taught myself to read when I was four. I'm sure that Kuydalls have not changed so much in all these years that they can't learn for themselves.

"Now, you, Susan—what do you want to start on?"

To say "I don't know" was something she simply could not do—not with Great-Aunt Hendrika looking at her that way and after hearing her talk about how Kuydalls knew so much. Only she was not a Kuydall— no matter what Grandma's name had been! She made a choice without any real thought, just to have a book in her hands—one of those Great-Aunt Hendrika had referred to as the *St. Nicholases*—

"And you—?" It was Mike's turn. He had no hesitation at all.

"I found something yesterday—its over on the desk." He pointed to the book Tucker had discovered, that had the ugly mask in it.

Great-Aunt Hendrika went to look. There was an expression of surprise on her face when she glanced up at Mike.

"Jacobus Kuydall's diary!" She frowned, then she shook her head. But Susan thought she was not shaking it at Mike.

"I did say anything here was for reading. And of course it is!" Her voice was firmer, almost as if she was making a promise—though to whom Susan did not understand. "You are certainly woefully lacking in a knowledge of family history. It is time you learned some. Very well, you have an hour." She looked at her watch again. "Then you must get dressed for church. We'll take the field walk so you'll get to see some more history—part of the past that belongs to you whether you are interested or not!"

Susan looked around for Tucker. He was no longer by the shelves. The table with the beads . . . No, he was not there either. In fact, Tucker had found an excellent place on a wide window seat, where he was hunched over, actually looking into the largest of the books, completely absorbed.

She found the large volume she had picked by chance was awkward to hold, and so she shared the desk with Mike—he on one side and she on the other—leafing through her choice to marvel at the queer clothes worn by the people in the illustrations: there were a lot of those. Great-Aunt Hendrika, perhaps considering her duty well done—at least for the hour she had mentioned—left them.

Mike made a queer noise, something between a snort and a laugh, which pulled Susan away from a story that had attracted her because of the title: "Lady Jane."

"Didn't the G.-A.," he looked across the flattened-out book he had opened, "say that one of the things we should learn was spelling?"

"Why?"

"Because the guy that wrote this was about the world's worst speller—or else they had a different kind of English in his day," Mike commented. "But he's got a lot to say. He lived here back in 1769—at least that's when he started writing this. And his mother was an Indian—an Oneida—an important person, too. Seems the women owned the land then. His father was from New York—another Jacobus Kuydall—who got a big grant, about this whole valley, but that was just what the colonists said. The Indians didn't argue, not until he moved in and made a deal with them. He married this princess or whatever they called her, and he set up a big trading post. Then he brought settlers in— some Scottish people. They were angry about what had happened in the old country and wanted to get out— didn't like their new king. And there were some Dutch, too—and even a couple of Swedes.

"This first Jacobus brought men from New York to build him this house—or part of it—and everyone thought it was great—like he was a king here. They used to hold big ceremonies with the Indians outside. He sent his two sons to England later on. The one who wrote this liked that, but his brother didn't. He was homesick, I guess. Jacobus talks about reading Latin— though he couldn't spell English straight. Has some Indian words mixed in too.

"His brother was Hendrik, and they don't seem to have been very good friends. When they got back from England, Jacobus hung around with some English who lived not far from here. But Hendrik was mad at the way the English were giving orders all over the place and that made more trouble between the brothers.

"This part of New York State was called 'the west' then 'cause people hadn't pioneered too far yet, and they didn't even know how big the whole country was. I've looked it up in another book—during the Revolution, Washington was always said to fight 'in the east,' and this place was considered way off the map, 'in the west.' Anybody who went to fight with Washington in the regular army was 'in the east.'

"Anyway Jacobus stayed here in the west and ran things at home. He was his father's favorite. But Hendrik was the oldest, and in those days the eldest son inherited everything by law."

Susan looked around the room slowly. Seventeen sixty-nine seemed a very long time ago. Was this already a library then? And had some of the same dark books been up on the shelves ever since?

"Children!" Mrs. Kingsley stood in the doorway. "Time to get ready for church."

Susan shut her book as did Mike, but Tucker might not have heard at all. When they both went over to the window seat they found him gazing at a picture of an Indian crouched behind a bush, watching a wall made of pointed logs, over the top of which showed the unmistakable coonskin cap of a frontiersman.

"Tucker—we've got to go." When he did not move Susan laid her hand, palm flat, over the picture.

"That was what they did—only it was morning—real early . . . " Tucker said slowly, without raising his head. "They snuck up—and then there was shooting and screaming—and—"

He gave his head a small shake. When he did seem to see Mike and Susan, he looked frightened. "They ran—and ran—and then it was all dark because the man put them—" Again he shook his head and slammed the book shut. "I don't know the rest!"

Mike picked up both books. "No more Indians, Tuck.

58

Just forget about Indians. There aren't any left around here any more. You've been imagining—"

Tucker's lower lip protruded. "They were bad—only the man—he was badder—and he wasn't an Indian! I don't want to remember any more."

"You don't have to," Susan was quick to assure him. "Come on, Tucker, we have to get ready for church."

He seemed willing enough and didn't protest when she got out his best slacks and a clean shirt and laid his jacket on the bed. He even let her run a comb through his upstanding thatch of hair.

Susan hoped they looked what she had once heard Lena back home call "respectable" when they met Great-Aunt Hendrika and Mrs. Kingsley in the lower hall. Great-Aunt was wearing a gray suit and hat and a frilly blouse. There was a pin on one lapel of her jacket, a big black leopard, only his spots were set with small sparkling stones. Mrs. Kingsley also had on a suit and hat, but they both lacked the frills that she wore in the house.

They walked down the gravel drive out into the road, but turned off into a side path as Great-Aunt Hendrika unlatched a gate that led them into the cemetery. A walk led straight across that toward the white church, but beside it stood a big block of stone quite tall, a plate of brownish-looking metal fastened to one side. Great-Aunt Hendrika stopped in front of it.

"In a few weeks," she told them, "it will be the two hundredth anniversary of the massacre. This was put up in 1880—the hundredth one. See there—" She pointed a gloved hand to some names on the metal plate.

"Johanna Kuydall, Carolus Kuydall, Florian Kuydall—" They were strange names and Susan found herself reading them aloud. There were a lot of other names, about twenty of them, but those three were at the top of the list.

"What happened?" Mike wanted to know.

Great-Aunt Hendrika looked—Susan could only think of one word—hard. As if her face were now a mask like the horrid one in the book Mike had found. "It was a very terrible thing," she said. "A man brought the enemy to raid his own friends—his own family. They burned the houses, killed—even his own blood. His name . . . " She hesitated and then went on. " . . . was Jacobus Kuydall. And he had a brother Hendrik, who was serving with Washington. Many of the families in the valley were divided, but Jacobus was the only one who brought death to his own people. There still are stories about him. You may even hear some of them. People in these small towns do remember—even today. Hendrik Kuydall made himself a beggar after the war trying to help those who survived that massacre. Still some of them hated and blamed him, because he had not been here to defend them. The Kuydalls did not live here for a long time afterward because of that. People are planning another ceremony on the two hundredth anniversary now. Still, Kuydall money set up this stone—and those three names at the top were Hendrik's children—"

The church bell began to ring, startling them. Susan took Tucker's hand, for he did not move on with the others, rather stood staring at the stone. This was too much, she thought. If Tucker did not stop hearing about Indians and killing—she wished she dared tell

60

Great-Aunt Hendrika so. Maybe Mother and Dad would find a house soon so they could get away from here.

Susan had seen some movies about war and read some books. It always happened somewhere else to other people, having nothing at all to do with the Whelans . . . The Whelans! That was it! They were not Kuydalls, no matter what Great-Aunt Hendrika said. They were Whelans, who had nothing at all to do with anything that had happened here two hundred years ago.

Church was all right. They sang some of the hymns Susan knew, and the minister had a nice smile. He came up to the big pew after the service to speak to Great-Aunt and Mrs. Kingsley about getting ready for the church canning bee and how pleased they were about all those extra jars and the apples Great-Aunt was contributing to make into sauce.

Tucker pulled at Susan's hand, jerking her impatiently toward the door, so she thought it best to get him out. Mike followed. There were some boys his age and a couple of girls near them. One of them smiled and Susan was so flustered she did not smile back in time. No one spoke to them.

They were outside walking slowly, waiting for Great-Aunt Hendrika and Mrs. Kingsley to catch up, when Eloise came by. There was another girl with her and two boys—big ones. One had a school sweater, which had a bright letter, white on red, under his jacket. The girl with Eloise looked at the Whelans with a round-eyed stare, as if there was something queer about them, while the boy in the sweater whispered to her and then laughed in a loud way Susan did not like. Mike didn't either—she saw him turn red.

"Ghosts set to get you, kid?" the big boy demanded of Mike. "Better get your running shoes on, maybe you can beat the rap this time. Heard it yet?" He began to chant: "A curse on thee, who Jacobus' blood be." He laughed again, and the other boy joined in, even though the strange girl pulled at his sleeve, her face redder than just the cold could make it.

Eloise snapped out of one corner of her mouth, "Shut up, Lew! If my aunt hears you . . . "

He laughed again. "Yeah? What's she going to do? She don't own me—and she sure can't shut up the town. Folks have been talking already. Three kids—Kuydalls—and you know what they say happened before where three of them got together here."

"What happened?" Mike took a step closer to the big boy. Mike was tall for his age, but he had to look up to see the boy's face. "Suppose you tell us."

"That's just it, kid. Nobody knows. It's the curse." He made his voice go deep. "Go and look over there—" He nodded toward the cemetery. "There are a lot of funny stories about the Kuydalls."

"We aren't Kuydalls," Mike answered with the same words Susan had thought earlier. "And what about a curse? That's something out of a comic book—"

"Come on, Lew." That was the other boy. "Here comes Mrs. Kingsley. She'll skin you alive if she hears you sound off—"

Lew glanced past the Whelans to the church, then laughed and shrugged. "I haven't said anything that isn't known. Coming, Eloise?"

"No, I've got to get home. My aunt'll see to that. Thanks, Laura, I had a swell time. See you all." She was plainly eager to have the three move on.

Mike was not satisfied. "What's this curse business?" he demanded of her. "You told Tucker about it—now tell us."

"Just an old story—doesn't mean anything," she said hurriedly. "Oh, Aunt Martha, Mrs. Whitman wants you to call her—something about baking extra cookies. The Ladies' Aid didn't get promise of enough." She walked with Mrs. Kingsley, and Mike was forced to step aside, joining Susan and Tucker as Great-Aunt Hendrika came along more slowly, talking to another lady. Once more Susan heard, "Auction—come early . . ."

She was glad they did not go back through the cemetery, but took a longer way along the road. Tucker kept picking up leaves—early fallen from some of the trees but already bright-colored. There was a crispness in the air. Susan pulled her jacket more tightly about her.

"What do you suppose they meant?" she asked Mike.

"I don't know but I am sure going to find out," he answered with determination. "From what the G.-A. said, Jacobus and Hendrik split over the revolution and Jacobus brought an Indian raiding party down while his brother was off fighting in the east. I guess that would make anyone mad enough to curse him. But what it's got to do with us—that we've got to find out."

Tucker joined them, his hands full of leaves. "What

63

makes them red and yellow?"he asked, and Susan was so thankful that he did not mention Indians or other horrors that she admitted freely she did not know, but perhaps Great-Aunt Hendrika did. Tucker shot a glance over one shoulder to where she stood, still talking to the lady, then lost interest in leaves as a squirrel ran along the wall, popped into a hole, and was gone.

"I sure wish I had a good old dog—"

"Digby," Susan said before she thought, and then was horrified at what she had done.

Tucker looked scornful. "Digby's gone. He's with *them*."

Oh no, Susan thought, not that again. "Wait until we get to Utica," she told him hurriedly. "We'll have a house there and you can get a dog—"

"Yes. Not here." He shook his head. "*They* might get him, too. Look—Mike—a jet!"

He pointed skyward. There was indeed a tail of white across the sky marking the path of the plane too high for them to see. A jet in the air, and two hundred years ago Indians coming out of the woods in the early morning to kill— In the early morning? Now why had she thought that? She had not heard Great-Aunt Hendrika say so. No, it had been Tucker, when he looked at the picture in the book. Yet the idea of an attack in the early morning seemed so plain that she was somehow certain it could be true. No more Indians! No more Kuydall curses!

Great-Aunt Hendrika caught up with them at last and Susan, frantically hunting a subject as far from her thoughts as possible, asked about the auction of her cousin Hester's things.

It was to be quite an event she learned. In the first place it was also in a way a Kuydall affair. Great-Aunt's cousin had been a Kuydall—Hester Kuydall—and she and Great-Aunt Hendrika had inherited the rights to the big house, to be shared equally. Only Hester did not like living in it, because one of her brothers had died there and she herself had been very ill when visiting it. Later, her own young son had died at the manor suddenly. Cousin Hester had lived in another house on the other side of town. Now she was dead, too, and all the things in her house were going to be sold at auction. The money would go to the church. Many of the things she had owned were old—antiques—and they expected quite a crowd to turn up, especially with good weather. The Ladies' Aid was going to sell lunches and it was a big occasion for the town.

"We'll go," Great-Aunt Hendrika said, as if promising a treat. "There may be something your mother might fancy for her new home. I know she is interested in old things. And she has a birthday in November, hasn't she? You might think of looking around for a present there, Susan. I can remember some quite nice bits of glass and china—not so old that they would attract dealers, but pretty. And of course they are family things, too."

Chapter

5

LUCKILY TUCKER APPEARED TO FOR-
get Indians during the next two
days. In the library he had found several books with
queer old pictures. There was one called *Cheerful Cats*,
another about *Brownies*. Ignoring the printing he followed the adventures of these quietly as Susan and
Mike dipped into their new way of school. Mike was
taking notes as he read, but Susan, who had never
particularly enjoyed reading, traced the Lady Jane
story through two volumes of the *St. Nicholas* and
then tackled *What Katy Did*.

On Tuesday morning they were again joined by
Great-Aunt Hendrika at breakfast and told they were
to attend the auction. The whole household, except for
Erasmus and Josiah, was to go. Great-Aunt Hendrika
considered this a part of Kuydall history and necessary
to their education.

"Not many of the old families are left," she said as she helped Mrs. Kingsley pack a big cardboard box with layers of cookies and cupcakes each in a sandwich bag. "The last of the McGregors—old Amos—died two years ago. There are still Vandusters and Grahams . . ." She shook her head. "Not much in the valley to hold our young people. They've been leaving now for a generation or more. They come back sometimes for a summer visit, and that's it. Houses are sold to summer people. Thank goodness there are a few round about who appreciate old things and are willing to preserve them. But the new families aren't native stock—"

Mrs. Kingsley sniffed. "Fancy horses and a swimming pool—and that tennis court they put in at the McGregor house. Wanting to nose into village business, too. We can do without most of 'em."

Great-Aunt Hendrika shook her head. "That's just it, Martha, we can't. At least, if they do take an interest, we won't have some kind of a housing project going up—like ugly mushrooms overnight. Those Allens who took over the McGregor house have done an excellent restoration job and they are proud of the place—put it in better order than it has been in for fifty years or more. I hope that Hester's home is as well cared for by these Hendersons. It needs a roof job badly. She just would not bother about the house the past year or so. Said as how it would outlast her and that was all that was necessary. Of course it isn't a Kuydall house—but it was built in 1800 and the Cannons brought in an architect from New York then to plan it."

They drove along the road on which the manor stood, heading into open country. There was other traffic. Great-Aunt Hendrika tooted her horn and waved at several cars, which signaled back. It was only eight in the morning, but it was going to be a good day. Susan settled in her corner seat and, sure they did not have a long drive before them, felt a little excited.

They turned into a field of parked cars. Great-Aunt Hendrika helped Mrs. Kingsley take out the big cardboard boxes of freshly baked things, while Eloise carried a lidded pot filled with three pies set in layers.

"Go on." Great-Aunt shooed the children ahead. "Look around. The things are all numbered and you can see what will come up for auction when the sale begins. Lucky this is a good day, they can bring most of the stuff out in the yard where people can see it better."

"A lot of folks have been seeing." Mrs. Kingsley sounded snappish. "People came out from town last Thursday and Friday just to poke around. Most of them just plain curious. Well, now, there's Sarah Bates, she has most things right under her hand—"

The food, Great-Aunt, Mrs. Kingsley and Eloise went in one direction, as the Whelans stood together looking around.

"It must be like a garage sale," Susan ventured. They had had one of their own two weeks before they had moved.

"Bigger," Mike commented. "Look at all the furniture!" He pointed to the front of the house at chairs, tables, sofas, beds which had been taken apart, cupboards, and some things so large and heavy Susan wondered how they had ever been carried out of the plain red brick house. People were prowling round among the furniture, turning chairs up to examine their legs, squatting down to look at the undersides of tables. Others sat around waiting for the show to begin. There were big cartons piled with books, dishes, and all kinds of odds and ends lined up along the edge of the porch.

Nobody spoke to the Whelans, and they were hesitant about venturing into the area where all the things were piled up and waiting. But what Great-Aunt Hendrika had said about finding something for Mother's birthday flashed into Susan's mind.

"Hey—look there, Tuck. What do you think of that?" Mike pointed to the gathering of furniture. Standing, dusty and dim of paint, between a table and two chairs was a pony. No, Susan took a second look. It was a wooden horse, with a carved, curly mane. There was a wooden saddle on its back, faintly streaked with faded red and gold paint, and from its half open mouth hung tattered ends of reins.

"It's from a merry-go-round." Susan hurried after the boys as Tucker, taking one look, started running. However, when she got close enough she saw that it was mounted on rockers, its hoofs—three of them— planted firmly in those supports. A fourth foot, a hind one, had been broken off and the rocker there was also cracked.

Tucker caught at the horn of the saddle and was making an effort to scramble up. The horse tottered and would have fallen against the table.

"You kids—cut it out! Get away from there!" A young man bore down upon them, swinging one arm to warn them off.

"We're sorry," Susan said hurriedly. "Tucker never

69

saw a horse like that before—"

"Well, see he keeps his hands off it. That's a special item."

"Does it cost a lot?" Mike was restraining Tucker with difficulty.

"You can just bet it will, kid. Not many of those left. Two of the dealers have it marked special in their catalogues. One of them said he could get a thousand or more for it from some collector."

Mike whistled and took a firmer hold on Tucker. "Nothing doing," he told his brother. "Look, there's a barn. Let's go and see what's there."

Tucker's face was turning red and Susan did not see what she or Mike could do if he really lost his temper.

"There's a dog!" Mike pointed to a small brown and white puppy playing in the trampled grass. Tucker swung away at once from the battered rocking horse. Then he was off, Mike fast behind him.

Susan lingered to ask a question of the big young man who seemed to know so much about things.

"Is everything going to be so expensive?"

He grinned at her. "Thinking to pick yourself up a bargain or two, sister? You look over there . . . " He gestured at the cartons piled on the porch. "Some of them won't even be put up for bidding. Harve says they came out of the attic where the church ladies packed 'em. They're like grab bags—the ladies thought that was a good idea. All the dealers will be after the big stuff—china and glass mostly; they don't want that kind of thing. Who knows, you might find yourself a real treasure."

She could not be sure whether he was making fun

of her or not, and just then someone yelled, "Hal!" and he went off. Susan moved toward the cartons he had pointed out.

They looked awfully dusty and dirty. Some had old books in them. She lifted the lid of one carton and saw a box filled with pieces of material cut in squares— patches. Maybe someone had once started to make a quilt and then never finished it. The pieces were trimmed. Pieces of lace or braid, sometimes both, had been cut out and sewn across one corner of each piece. They were not all calico, like Mother's friend Mrs. Platt used to make the quilts she worked on. Some looked like dusty velvet or wool. Susan picked up the top ones, only to discover that they had been fastened together by pieces of faded tape so they made a string of squares. She did not want to take them all out, but she wondered about them.

There was a second box beneath the one with patches. It had once been painted by someone to look like wood, and it was badly broken across the top. Stuffed along the edge, to fill up the rest of the carton, were loose printed pages, all yellowed and spotted. And at one corner was something wrapped up in a piece of frayed cloth. Susan poked a finger all the way through the cloth trying to see what was inside. It looked like a little tree made of china, with several branches. A couple of them were painted with flowers and a butterfly. It was strange—and unusual. She did not know what it really was, but suddenly Susan wanted it. She squatted down to read black markings on the outside of the box.

"Church fund, grab bag. Two dollars."

71

Maybe the tree thing was broken. And who would want the pieces of the quilt or whatever they were. But two dollars for a grab bag. She did not know what was in the box painted to look like wood either. Susan had never taken a chance like this—but it might be fun.

"Found something interesting? Oh, you're Susan Whelan, aren't you?"

Susan nearly lost her balance, sitting on her heels the way she was, as she looked up with a start.

"I'm Mrs. Reevers, we met at church. But I think you were meeting so many people there you might not remember." The lady looked a little like Mother, her hair covered with a scarf, a windbreaker on, and a smiling face. Susan did *not* remember her, but she smiled back. Mrs. Reevers was more like someone from home than anybody she had met so far.

"Yes, I'm Susan. This grab bag box—how do you buy it?"

"You pay me." Mrs. Reevers laughed. "This is my part of the auction. The money will go into a special church fund we want to raise for young people's programs. Maybe the kind you would enjoy."

Susan fumbled in the front of her jacket to get her wallet. She counted out four quarters left from her last allowance and then ten dimes that she had shaken out of her piggy bank before she packed it. "I'm going to buy this." She laid one hand on the box. Then she smiled. "Maybe I'm going to be lucky!"

Mrs. Reevers smiled back. "Do you know, I have a feeling that you are! I do know that there are some surprises packed away in most of these. There was so much up in the attic, and the ladies who sorted it all out finally thought that there was just too much to bother with, so they pushed as much as they could in each box and left it to be priced. Thank you, Susan." She dropped the money in a bag she had. "Let me know if you got a surprise."

"Oh, I will!" Susan picked up the box. It was rather heavy. She wondered what could be in the bottom of it as she carried it carefully to the car and put it on the floor in the back. Then she went off to hunt Mike and Tucker, finding them playing with the puppy and talking to two boys.

Susan drifted on to where the church ladies were putting out paper plates, getting ready to sell lunch to any who had not brought their own. The auction was beginning. For a while Susan listened to it. The man who was selling the things talked so fast and so loud he was hard to understand—and there were some people in the front row who looked quite dressed up and who bid on the furniture. Perhaps they were dealers. The rocking horse, to her surprise, did bring in seven hundred dollars—even though it was broken.

She cornered Mike later on to explain about the grab bags and after a while saw him poking around the ones with books in them. Then everyone took time out—Susan thought that the man who was doing the talking certainly needed that—and had lunch. There were sandwiches and milk and lots of different kinds of cookies, pie pieces and slices of cakes, which they ate picnic fashion.

Shortly after lunch Great-Aunt Hendrika and Mrs.

Kingsley packed up, saying it was time to go home. Great-Aunt Henrika shook her head as she climbed into the car.

"I don't know how all those dealers got wind of the sale. Good for the church, yes. But they outbid the rest of us. I wanted that sewing table. Mama used to have that up in her room when I was little—but three hundred dollars!"

"They weren't so free with their money when it came to the kitchen stuff." Mrs. Kingsley was quite triumphant. "Got me that rolling pin that presses out Christmas cookies. I always fancied that." She patted the wooden roller with its deeply indented patterns. "Next Christmas I'll try Ettie's recipe and see just how good it works. What's all this?"

She had opened the car door and there sat Susan's carton—another beside it with some books on top.

"Grab bag boxes," Susan said quickly. "This one's mine. I guess the other is Mike's. Mrs. Reevers said they were full of things out of the attic."

Mrs. Kingsley sniffed. "Trash mainly, I suppose. Where are those brothers of yours?"

"They're coming." Great-Aunt Hendrika had been waving and now the boys were running from the barn. "Let's get out of here before we are caught in a jam. The sale went quicker than they thought it would. Look at them loading up those vans. Well, it made plenty for the church and that is what Hester wanted."

"That's a good dog," Tucker said. "His name's Butch and he lives with Johnny. He's a dog to go hunting with. Johnny's going to train him to hunt."

"Dogs," Great-Aunt Hendrika said as she got behind

the wheel of the car, "are all right—in their proper place. Which is *not* in a house! Where's Eloise?"

"She said as how she was staying on for a little while—wants to help Mrs. Reevers—she and Laura. Seems that Susan here was not the only one to fancy those grab boxes and they are having a pretty good sale of them. Guess people are always ready to take a chance on finding a treasure. Even though they end up mostly with trash. The Prestons will drop her off by four."

Susan carried her box inside when they got home. Getting it upstairs was another matter, for it was awkward to handle. Also Tucker was talking more and more about a dog, until she was certain that if Digby did not return, they were going to have another invisible puppy in his place sooner or later.

She heard Mike trying to interest Tucker in what might be in his own grab box, only to be asked scornfully who wanted a lot of old dirty books.

They had just reached the upper hall when Susan tripped and went down on her knees, trying hard not to drop the box. Some of the loose pages that had been put in for packing fell out, and the top box, with the squares of cloth, lost its cover so that the patches trailed along the carpet.

"Great-Grandma Lutie's dress string!" Great-Aunt Hendrika had followed them upstairs. Now she stooped to pick up the squares, stretching out a string that was quite long.

"There's Grandma McAdams' wedding dress—and her infare dress which was almost as important then. It was the dress you wore to church the first Sunday after your wedding. And this is a piece of the dress she had on when Grandpa Kuydall proposed . . . "

To Susan's surprise Great-Aunt Hendrika sat down on the floor to examine each patch in turn. She was smiling, and now and again she nodded as if she had met a friend she remembered.

"How we loved this," she said. "Mama used to get it out if we had to stay in bed with a cold, then she would tell us the story of each one. Why, some of these dresses must go back to Lucy Kimble's time—far more than a hundred years ago. She was the one who began it, I believe. She was a beautiful dressmaker, and every time she made a dress that was to be worn for some special occasion, she took a piece of the material, sewed the trimming across it and kept it. Then Great-Grandma Lutie and Grandma added to it in their day, too. It is a history in itself. I had forgotten all about it. But I haven't forgotten the stories—not when I see this again!"

She began to fold it up, square against square, and handed it back to Susan.

"This is certainly rightfully yours, Susan—since you are the eldest daughter in your generation! In fact the only one—" For a moment she lost her smile and sat staring down at her hands, which now rested on her knees. Then she glanced up again.

"What other luck did you have, Susan?"

The wadded papers, which had held the box tightly packed, had all been pulled out, for Susan was eager to see the little piece of china in the corner. She unwrapped the old piece of cloth, which pulled apart easily in her fingers, to discover this really was like a small tree—a thick stem for trunk, then four branches each upheld in a different direction. The base was a round plate like a saucer from a doll tea set, and, though the china was very dusty and dirty, you could see more flowers and butterflies painted on it. What it might be still puzzled Susan.

"A ring tree!" Great-Aunt Hendrika said. "You never saw one before, Susan? These were meant to be put on the dressing table to hang up rings you were not wearing." She touched the tip of one branch. "I don't remember seeing this, but it is pretty."

"Mom could hang her watch on that." Mike had returned from his own room into which he had carried his grab box. "Bet she'd like it, Sue. It's old, isn't it?" he asked.

"Old and perhaps a good piece, too."

There was only one other thing in the carton, the other box painted to look like wood. This was so broken that Susan was afraid it would come apart in her hands as she lifted it out. Great-Aunt Hendrika leaned forward a little and Susan heard her gasp.

She looked up and saw Great-Aunt reaching out as if to take the box from her, but she did not actually touch it. Her smile was quite gone and she looked odd, almost as if she were afraid or sick.

"So . . . Hester kept those after all. At least they were gone from here." Great-Aunt Hendrika got up and stood, still looking down at the box. "No, that is all just superstition!" She spoke very firmly and harshly. "There is nothing in such silly stories—nothing." But she was no longer the person who had been so pleased at finding the dress patches. Now she turned abruptly and went down the hallway in the direction of her own room in the added-on wing, leaving Susan sitting surprised, the broken box in her hands. Mike stared after his great-aunt, but Tucker took no notice. He had been quietly putting together the crumpled, yellow sheets that had been jammed in to fill up the carton. Though it was certainly *not* Tucker's way to help clean anything up.

"What's in that box?" Mike swung back to his sister.

She lifted off the broken cover, almost afraid to do so. There was such a strange feeling inside her—as if she were about to let out what should be carefully kept in a cage. She found herself looking down at a piece of stout cardboard, which she carefully raised. It was not as badly damaged as the box. Below it was a mass of color—surprisingly bright color—in contrast to the dark and faded box.

"Paper dolls," Susan said, wonderingly. She and Francie had had some last summer—a whole wedding party set. But these—she did not want to touch them— not with dirty hands. These were not just printed on paper. Instead, their faces were painted, and—yes— there were wisps of real hair glued to their heads! They were like pictures of people—real people.

"Paper dolls!" Mike gave one scornful look and lost interest. "What is there about a bunch of paper dolls to set the G.-A. off that way?"

Susan wanted to unpack them all. She'd wash her hands, then lay them out on her bed where she could really see them. They were so unusual. When she looked down at the faces of the three lying on top, a girl and two boys, it was as if she saw old snapshots of real people.

"They're different." Susan picked up the box carefully. She would have to find something better to keep them in. A long time ago someone had painted this box to look like a big wooden chest, but it was almost completely broken now and useless.

"Indians . . . "

Tucker's comment certainly had nothing to do with what she held. He had stopped piling up the brittle old pieces of paper to look closely at one he had just straightened out. On it was a picture, crudely drawn in pen and ink by someone who was not much of an artist. But it was an Indian right enough. And he had his hand twisted in the hair of a woman who was on her knees, her mouth wide open as if she were screaming for help.

" 'Dastardly murder . . . ' " Mike pulled that sheet of paper away from Tucker. It tore so he had to hold it together with both hands. " 'The Murders in Candiaga Valley'; 'Death of Mary MacRae'; 'The Curse of the Kuydalls as spoken by one of the victims . . . ' " he read. "Tucker, let's see that stuff!"

He knelt and started sorting out the pile of papers Tucker had gathered together. "Say, these are all parts of a book—all about the massacre here!" He was reading a sentence here and there as he sorted. "Let me have them, Tucker."

Susan gathered up her own things—the ring tree,

the dress pieces, and the box of dolls.

"No more Indians," she said. "If you get Tucky started off again, it is all your fault, Mike. I won't have anything to do with it."

Oddly enough Tucker did not appear to be too excited this time. Instead he was sitting cross-legged, much as Great-Aunt Hendrika had done earlier, watching Mike sort out the pieces of paper into piles.

Susan carried her armload into her bedroom, went to wash thoroughly, and came back to examine those interesting paper dolls. Mike had bundled up one package of the crumpled leaves. Tucker waited until he had finished, then reached for those his brother had discarded.

"You don't want those dirty old things," Susan said quickly.

Tucker looked up at her. "Might," he replied, gathering them very close to his chest. Before she could argue it out with him he marched into his room and actually slammed the door behind him.

"Mike—don't let him—" she was beginning, but her older brother did not appear to be listening to her at all.

"This is a story—all about the Kuydalls and the valley massacre," he said excitedly. "There is something about the curse, too. This was written later—must have been about the time when they put up that stone in the cemetery." He clutched his share of papers as tightly as Tucker had done.

Susan shook her head determinedly. "I don't want to hear any more about it and I don't think you should talk about such things before Tucky either! It's upsetting!" Why did she feel suddenly so cold? Why did she want to snatch those papers from Mike and tear them into little bits? She did not know. Only she wished to forget all about the Kuydalls and the valley, Indians and such things that were not part of this real world now at all.

Chapter
6

THERE WERE, SUSAN DISCOVERED when she laid the dolls out carefully on her bed, four sets, each quite different from the others. Those on top were made of heavy cardboard that had been carefully painted, while their faces seemed to have been cut from old photographs, tinted and pasted onto the bodies, with bits of real hair glued in place. There were three of them and the clothes they wore, while unusual to Susan, were not so very strange.

Under a second sheet of cardboard lay three more dolls. These also had faces that could have come from photographs but much older ones. The dresses for the girl, the clothes for the boys, reminded Susan of pictures from the older copies of the *St. Nicholas* magazines. There were frills, flounces and ruffles on the girl's dresses, and her hair was in bangs across her forehead, falling into curls on her shoulders.

The third set of dolls was even more strange. They had been made of what Susan believed must be many thicknesses of stout paper glued together. The boys wore very odd-looking clothing and the girl—her dresses were so full that they stuck out on all sides and she wore some kind of pants underneath that came down to her ankles. Her hair was parted in the middle and drawn back to her ears over which it hung in bunches of short curls. The faces of these three had not been clipped from old photos but were very delicately drawn in ink and then painted.

The fourth set—the last—was three children again. These dolls had no extra clothing to be put on and taken off. They were already dressed. Susan believed they were made of thin skin stretched over a wooden base and then painted with care. Their faces were so faded and smudged by time that it was very hard to see any features at all, and one could only judge by the clothing, also painted on, whether they were boy or girl. The girl wore a long dress that hid all but small humps that might be the toes of slippers. Over that she had a full apron, and around her shoulders a kind of shawl or scarf knotted in front, its end left to dangle. Most of her hair had been pulled up under a puffy cap. The boys had pants that came only to their knees. Below those they wore long stockings and square-toed shoes. Their shirts had small ruffles down the front, and their coats must once have been blue. Their hair was long—tied back at the nape of their neck, as Susan could see when she turned them over, for they were as finished on the back as on the front.

Somehow she did not like to touch this last set. Perhaps it was the feel of the leatherlike stuff that covered their bodies, perhaps it was because she could not see their faces clearly—as if they were in hiding. Hiding? Susan shook her head, as she put them hurriedly to one side. What had made her think of that?

The set with painted faces she studied more closely. There were two dresses for the girl made of small scraps of lace paper and some thin silk, which split a little when she touched it. One of the boys had a kilt and a jacket to wear—and then what looked almost like a girl's dress, with trousers gathered in tightly at the ankles. The other, taller one had long white trousers and a black short coat and a soldier-suit in blue. Susan looked carefully at their faces. They were not made to be pretty. The older boy had a scallop of hair down over his forehead which made him look rather cross. She could almost imagine that he was preparing to stick his tongue out at someone. The girl's small mouth was rather squeezed together and her nose gave the impression of turning up at the end.

It was when Susan turned them over to see if they also were finished on the back as well as on the front that she noticed very small writing, faded and brown. She took them nearer the window to try and make out what it said.

Even the writing was different, curly yet quite plain to read when she got the full light on it.

" 'Emily, Jethro, Orrin'. " She read the names aloud. Jethro was the taller boy doll.

Emily! Susan's attention went from the doll she held to the picture her mother had called a sampler. Was that—had this doll belonged once to *Emily Kimble*?

She returned the three to the bed and took up the next set, with their photograph faces and wisps of hair. There was certainly no mistaking that they had been meant to resemble real people. Quickly Susan turned them over. Yes, writing here also—a little darker and bolder.

"Richard"—that was the bigger boy; "Tod"—the younger one; "Bessie"—the girl.

Their clothing was fastened together with loops of thread. Bessie's dress had bows, pleats, and pieces of lace. For Richard, there was a suit like a soldier—an odd-looking soldier. Tod had a jacket and long trousers and a tasseled cap for his head.

Then came the newest set of dolls. These too had names: "Hester, James, and Orrin," Susan read. Hester's long hair could be covered by two big-brimmed hats, and the waistline of her dresses was set low. The dresses were also covered with lace—some of paper, some tiny bits of very fine real material, and tissue paper. James's trousers were short and tight fitting and his coat looser. There was a second suit with a khaki-colored coat, a wide brimmed hat and pants tucked into boots. Orrin had a sailor suit with a straw hat and another with a pair of the same tight-looking trousers that his brother wore.

Though she had pushed away the first three stiff dolls, Susan had not felt the same queer desire to get the rest out of sight so quickly. They had been real people once—in a way, that is. At least they had been made to look like real people. And they had lived a long time ago, of that she was sure. Susan wanted to know more about them. Who had made them all with such care and kept them? She was sure that they had not all been made at the same time. The dresses of the second set were so fragile she was afraid to touch them. That set must be very old.

"Emily, Jethro, Orrin," she recited the names again. "Richard, Bessie, and Tod, and Hester, James, Orrin—"

Hester! That was the name of the lady who had died—out of whose attic the doll box had come. Was she *this* Hester? Susan stared down at the family of dolls. Hester certainly was not a very pretty girl. Her fringe of hair was not in careful curls and her nose looked too big for her thin face. She was not smiling. In fact—Susan surveyed the entire collection of paper people quickly—none of them were smiling, nor did they look happy. James lay beside Hester, his face very thin and his eyes big and rather sleepy-looking. Susan thought that he looked ill.

Why would anyone want to make paper dolls like real people?

"Why?" She asked that aloud. "Why were you made, Emily, Jethro, Orrin One, Richard, Bessie, Tod, Hester, James and Orrin Two?"

"Orrin Two what?" Mike had come to the door she had left a little open.

"Orrin Two—him." Susan pointed to the second doll. "They all have their names on the back. And they are awfully old, I think—these—they have faces from photographs . . . And they've real hair pasted on. They're made to look like real people who lived once."

Suddenly Susan had a strange feeling of uneasiness. No use sticking them back in the same box. It was too

86

broken to handle. But she did not want to look at them any longer.

She circled around Mike, who had come to the side of the bed and was bending over to get a closer look of those faces she had indicated. In her bottom bureau drawer was a box holding her best blouse, the one she had not worn yet. Susan slid it out, still wrapped in tissue paper, and brought its white container back to the bed.

The wooden ones first. She had a strange feeling that she must put them back in the same order in which they had lain for so many years. As she reached for them, Mike moved closer.

"What are those? They look a lot different."

"Some more dolls—but they have their clothes on tight. And . . . and . . . they're ugly." She hurried to settle them in the blouse box and cover them over. Then one by one she returned the three other families into storage in the proper order. For families she was sure they were—brothers and sisters.

"Queer looking lot," Mike commented. "Hey—I've seen a uniform like that!" He was pointing to the one worn by the James of the last family. "That's like what the cavalry wore—in the First World War. Before they stopped riding horses and went into tanks and things."

"When did they do that?" Susan wanted to know. It might give her some idea of how old that family was.

"I don't know, but I'll look it up. Anyway what do a lot of old dolls matter? Listen, Susan—I found out about the curse! It's a real spooky story."

Susan put the cover on the box and shut it in her drawer. She rubbed her hands up and down the sides of her jeans. Ever since she had handled the oldest dolls she had felt dirty. As if she wanted to scrub with a lot of soap and very hot water.

"What's spooky?"

"Those torn-up sheets of paper—well, they were part of a book—a paperback. Funny, I didn't know there were paperbacks way back then. But somebody named Kimble wrote it and it was published in 1880. Just when they were having that big hundred year thing about the massacre, which the G.-A. was talking about. When they put that monument up and all. Anyway this Kimble made a real scary story of it.

"Seems like it wasn't all Indians who came raiding into the valley . . . In fact, one of the Indian chiefs pulled his men out when he found what the Tories were going to do. He said that the people here had always been friends to the Indians. So they used blue-eyed Indians for most of the raid—with some others who were not part of the regular tribe."

"Blue-eyed Indians?"

"That's what they called whites who dressed up and painted themselves like Indians. They were the worst kind according to this Kimble guy and they really were killers—wild men. Well, you remember there were two brothers, Jacobus and Hendrik Kuydall. Hendrik had inherited this house when their father died. He was the one who took the Revolutionary side and was with Washington in the east. His wife and his three children had been living in the east too, but he sent them back here to live. Hendrik and Jacobus were part Indian because their mother was an Oneida. It's in that old diary. Hendrik was sure that, because of his

Indian blood and the fact that he had always lived in peace with the Indians and this valley was off the main trail for raiders, everything would be safe here for his family.

"His wife—her name was Betje—she knew a lot about helping sick people. That night there was a woman down in the village who was having a baby and was in difficulties, so they sent for Mrs. Kuydall to come and help. She left the three children, Johanna, Carolus, and Florian, with two servants and went. No one had any idea that there was going to be any attack.

But Jacobus was mad—I mean really out of his head. The war had been going against the Tories in this part of the country, and he had always been jealous—or so this Kimble said—of his brother Hendrik. He thought this house should have been his. So he decided to loot the manor and get some money and stuff he was sure was hidden here, then beat it up to Canada.

"Also he wanted to make a big name with the British and maybe get a good deal in the north if he came back with a lot of booty and captives. So he planned the raid. Only, the Indians weren't ready to back him up. By that time he was willing to take anyone who would help him, and he apparently didn't care about what might happen to anyone here.

"From what the people could discover afterwards, he and his gang sneaked up at night and attacked in the early morning. Mrs. Kuydall was on her way home and saw enough to make her take to the woods to try to get to her house the back way. She crawled into a hollow log to hide when the raiders came close, then got stuck and couldn't get out till later. They really gave it to the valley—killed people and looted and burned. Jacobus and some others came straight to this house. He killed the servants—or some of his gang did—and the children disappeared. They were kidnapped—going to be used for ransom everyone thought. But, when Hendrik came home and tried to find out what had happened to them and Jacobus later, there was just no news at all. Everybody believed the Indians—or Jacobus' gang—really killed them because they couldn't keep up. Raiders used to do that to people.

"The people in the village found out about Jacobus and the fact that he wanted the loot from the manor and had done all the killing to get it. There was one woman who lost her two children, and she was hurt so bad that she was ill a long time. Maybe she went mad or something. She was supposed to have the evil eye, so she made up that rhyme about Kuydall and said that children who shared Jacobus' blood would *always* have trouble hanging over them—that they might die when they were the same age as the children she'd lost.

"Hendrik had another son and daughter later. His wife wouldn't live in this house so they moved to New York. The daughter married a man named Kimble, and later her son took over this house. Then back in 1840 one of the Kimbles had three children. People had sort of forgotten what the woman had predicted by then. But one of the children, the youngest, took a fever and raved about an ugly thing chasing him. That made people remember the old story. He died soon and so did his sister Emily, while the older boy

90

was sick for a long time. The Kimbles went back to New York with the Kuydalls and only came here in summertime. Because the curse was only supposed to happen at the same time of year as the raid."

Susan had settled down on the edge of the bed to listen. Mike was right—this was a spooky story and he was telling it to sound like one of those movies that they were not allowed to go to—the horror ones.

"This woman who did the cursing was part Indian, too. She was supposed to belong to False Faces. They were a secret society. Everybody wore these big masks and no one knew who anyone was."

"Like that picture in the diary!"

Mike nodded. "Yes, what I read about it there says that Jacobus was interested in a lot of the old Indian beliefs. I don't know whether he ever got in with the False Faces. But he had seen some of the masks and that one in the book was one he drew."

"So that's the curse . . . " Susan said slowly. "But there were a lot of illnesses in those days and people died from them . . . "

"Yes. Only once you get a spooky story started, it sticks. The Kimble who wrote this book finished with the celebration coming up in 1880, saying that Kuydalls were going to set up the marker in the cemetery. The Kimbles were coming with the Kuydalls for the ceremony."

"Emily and Orrin and Jethro—and those older dolls," said Susan slowly. "Maybe the oldest ones of all were the Kuydalls who disappeared. And Emily and Orrin died. But there are two more families in the box, Mike. There's Richard and Bessie and Tod, then Hester,

James and another Orrin. What happened to them?"

"They must have come later. There's nothing about them in the book. But maybe we can find out. Maybe Jacobus wasn't the only one to keep a diary," Mike suggested. "Only how did the dolls get over to that other house?"

"This Hester—the one who died and left everything to the church," Susan said, "she was a cousin of Great-Aunt's, and she had a thing about this house. Great-Aunt wanted her to come back and live here but she wouldn't. Though if she was one of the family—"

"Sure that fits. You heard what G.-A. said about that sewing table, which belonged to her mother and turned up at the sale—the one she would have liked to have had. Things out of this house must have been taken to that one. We can find out a lot more by looking—"

Susan pleated the coverlet of the bed between her fingers.

"Do we really want to, Mike?"

"Why not?" he demanded in open surprise.

"Well, like you said, it's spooky. And if Tucker hears any of this—you know what can happen."

"We keep our mouths shut. I'll tell you what—you can help look in the library too, and in such a way that Tuck won't know what you are doing."

"How?"

"By doing just what you've been doing—going through those children's books. I noticed a lot of them have writing in the front saying birthday present to so and so—with a date—or Christmas to so and so with a date. You can find out those dates and the names that match and then—There's the Bible!"

"What Bible?"

"That big book in a box all to itself on the small shelf behind the door. I looked in the box Sunday and saw it. It's awfully old, has metal hinges. Also it's printed in Dutch—anyway, in some different language—part Latin, I think. Anyway they used to have sections in old Bibles where they put down when all the family were born, and when they got married, and when they died. If we find out some names and dates, we can look them up in that."

What Mike said made sense. Susan did not really want to try it, but she had no excuse. Once Mike got on the trail of something he followed it to the end. Other people in school might groan and moan over having to do a paper and look up a lot of things in the library—Mike went at it as if it were a puzzle game, and the harder it was the better he liked it.

After all, her part of looking in the fronts of books to see who they had belonged to was easy enough, something that would not get Tucker too interested or excited. She was certainly willing to do that much. In fact, it would be interesting. Now that she had the paper dolls, those long ago people seemed real, and it would be fun to see what kinds of books Emily, Bessie, and Hester had enjoyed the most.

They were summoned to supper, not in the kitchen as usual, but in the dining room where Great-Aunt Hendrika sat at the head of the table and there was an array of glass, china, and silver, such as Susan had seen only at dinner parties—times when the younger Whelans had eaten in the breakfast corner of the kitchen at home. Tucker squirmed in his chair, looking at the fine tablecloth, the number of forks, spoons, and the tall glass before him with an interest Susan mistrusted.

"Cousin Hester," Great-Aunt Hendrika began after Mrs. Kingsley had set a vast soup tureen before her and she was quickly and efficiently filling soup plates from its contents, "never used the Kuydall china. I have decided that it is best to enjoy beautiful things. This is another part of education, to learn how to cherish and enjoy the possessions of one's own family. We shall have at least one meal a week to do so."

She had set the ladle down and put out one hand to touch the thin stem of the water goblet before her, when a tremendous crack of thunder sounded from directly overhead.

Tucker's spoon slipped from his fingers to splash into the plate, sending a thin shower of soup onto the old linen. Susan gave a gasping cry as the lights abruptly went out.

"Stay right where you are!" Great-Aunt Hendrika's voice commanded. "This happens from time to time." There was a flicker of light, as if she had a lighter all ready, and it was touched to the nearest of the centerpiece candles. From that one, the spark advanced to the second, the third, and finally the fourth. Their light made a soft glow in the dark room, while outside the windows lightning flashed fiercely.

So they ate by candlelight and Susan tried very hard not to turn her head to peer into the dark corners of the room. She cowered every time the thunder rolled hard or the lightning crackled.

"Let us hope," Great-Aunt Hendrika said, "that the

current will be restored speedily. Though goodness knows we have candles enough, and there are the battery lamps for the bedrooms. We do not trust candles there."

The lights did not come on again before they finished dinner. Even if they had wanted to go delving in the library tonight, it was no use now. Susan wondered just how many stains were gathering around Tucker's place at the table. Perhaps it was just as well that Great-Aunt and Mrs. Kingsley could not see the results of this attempt to dine elegantly. At least so far as the youngest Whelan was concerned. She, herself, was so conscious of spilling something that she was almost afraid to take a full mouthful, or attempt to eat anything near the edge of the china plates.

The storm was furious. Mrs. Kingsley remarked that they were lucky it had held off long enough for the auction. She and Great-Aunt carried on an animated discussion about the buyers and the probable sum the church might expect while the three Whelans applied themselves wholly to eating.

It was Mrs. Kingsley who at last marshalled them into line at the foot of the stairs, handing Mike two of the round-footed, battery-run storm lamps, and Susan one which, when switched on, gave far more light than the candles had. Tucker was instructed not to "play with" the one intended for his room. The order would normally have brought an instant protest from him. But perhaps the storm and the darkness had a dampening effect, since he remained silent.

They went up the stairs and Mike obediently set one of his lamps on the bureau in Tucker's room, while Susan carried her own. In spite of the advantages of this light over the candles she was not happy and went once to both windows to pull down the shades against the storm.

She had shucked her T-shirt and jeans and had her robe wrapped around her when she looked up into the dusky mirror. Even in daylight the old glass had always been faintly murky, as if it were dirty though she knew that couldn't be true in any house over which Mrs. Kingsly had control. Tonight, in spite of the battery lamp, the upper right hand corner appeared even more dusky than usual. She was turning away, having no desire to see her own face peering back at her, when there was a movement in the glass.

Susan backed away from the bureau. Silly—nothing could flutter like that! Of course, maybe some draft had found its way in around a window to stir the edge of a curtain. She had *not* seen an oval outline of a great face with a lopsided mouth and blind holes for eyes! Mike with his spooky stories—

"Susie!" The call came between two rolls of thunder so she heard it. Tucker! She turned hurriedly away from the mirror to throw open her door. There was a path of light coming from his room. He had the door wide open, so that, as she hurried across into that picture-walled place, she had no trouble seeing Tucker himself. He huddled on the foot of the bed, staring at the far wall, and she had never known such a look on his face before. She had seen Tucker in a hot rage of anger, and in disappointment, and sometimes in full enjoyment. This was Tucker afraid—deathly afraid.

"Tucky!" She followed the direction of his stare.

There was only the wall with its mass of pictures. Where he stared was a garden scene with a small boy and a puppy apparently having a tug of war over a stick. The little boy was wearing clothes that looked much like those on one of the paper doll boys, but there was nothing in the least alarming about him.

"Susie . . . " As Susan came closer, Tucker made a lunge that carried his small body hard against hers. She caught him in her arms, staggering a little as his weight nearly sent her backwards to the floor. "Susie— I want to go home! I don't want to go with—*them*—not ever!"

Though she did not know what he meant, Susan understood that Tucker needed her, needed reassurance more than anything else.

"You don't have to go anywhere, Tucky. Unless—" A sudden thought of what might be comforting crossed her mind. This room was big and the storm very loud, not a time to be alone. "—unless you want to come in with me?"

Tucker burrowed his head tighter against her shoulder. His voice was very muffled.

"Please, Susie, oh, please!"

She pulled him with her, stopping only to catch up his lamp, and brought him out into the hall. Tucker hung onto her with both hands, refusing to let go, so that she closed his door with a definite kick and led the way back to her room under the roar of the rain and thunder.

Chapter

7

TUCKER CURLED UP IN SUSAN'S BED, his eyes closed. She believed he was keeping them squeezed shut. Susan had never seen her small and very determined brother so subdued before. As he had crawled into bed his eyes—wide open—had been big and staring, looking from one corner of her room to the other quickly, as if watching threatening shadows.

It was not easy for Susan herself to get to sleep. The storm seemed to go on forever, as she squirmed around in the portion of the bed Tucker left free, trying to make herself comfortable.

At last the thunder rumbled farther away. There were no more lightening flashes. Susan slipped out of bed to raise the shades at both windows—even though that did not give much light.

Back in bed again, she found herself listening. Not

for thunder anymore, rather for sounds within the house itself. Somehow the darkness changed things in a way she had never been aware of back home. This house was so old, there had been so many people here, there had been—

Susan pressed her hands tightly together. *NO!* She was not going to think about that family curse—she was not! Besides, that was a Kuydall story, it had nothing to do with the Whelans. She wanted to get up that very minute and dump the whole box of paper dolls out of the window, never think of them again. Instead she found herself saying, in a hissing whisper: "Johanna, Carolus, Florian, Jethro, Emily, Orrin, Richard, Bessie, Tod, Hester, James, and Orrin!" When she shut her eyes against the gloom of the room she could see all those paper faces. Even, this time, the faces of the three earliest ones, which had been so faded that before she could not make them out clearly.

Johanna had a round face, with a small, up-turned nose, her eyes were round, too—and her mouth was open. There was . . . Johanna was screaming!

Susan turned her head back and forth on the pillow, trying hard to shut that picture out of her mind—of Johanna's mouth opened to scream. Carolus was standing with his arms up—in his hands a queer gun so heavy that it took both hands to hold it steady and even then it wobbled. His mouth was tight shut, but his eyes were frightened—he was trying hard not to cry out. And little Florian—he had backed up against a rough stone wall. How she was seeing all this Susan could not have said—yet it was plain to her and she could not switch those faces off like the TV when it scared her. Florian crouched down a little, his body so stiff with fear he could not move at all . . .

NO!

"Susie!" That call broke the picture. She felt Tucker's small arms tightly around her as she sat up in bed.

"*They* came—Susie—*they* came!" Tucker's voice was harsh with fear. "*They*'re going to get us—*they* want us!"

Susan held Tucker as close as she could. "They're nothing but dolls," she said out of her dream, if that horrible picture had been a dream. "I saw them— they're nothing but dolls, Tucky! There's nothing to be afraid of." Only she was finding it very hard indeed to say that. Had bringing the dolls back here to this house made her dream? And—how had Tucker known what she was dreaming? For by this time she was sure, she had to be sure, it was only a dream. Could two people have the same dream?

"*They* never went away." Tucker paid no attention to what she said. "They just wait and wait and wait . . . " His voice trailed off. He was crying—not loud and demandingly as Tucker usually cried when he was hurt and wanted attention, but rather as if he was lost in a terrible dream of his own and had no hope of escaping from it.

"Tucker"—Susan drew a deep breath—"what are you talking about? Did you have a bad dream?"

"*They*—they went into the dark place and they waited—and no one came. Now they want to come out. They want to be helped." He gulped and sniffled between words.

"Tucker." She tried to make her voice as firm as she could. "Tell me—who are *they*?"

He jerked in her hold, loosed his own clutch on her, fought against her grip on him. She was forced by the sudden fury of his struggle to let him go.

"I want to go home!" Now his voice held the old familiar demanding note. "I want to go home! I hate this place!"

"Sue, Tuck—what are you two doing? Trying to yell down the house?" Light showed from the hall as Mike sent the door flying open, standing there with one of the storm lamps in his hand.

"What's Tuck doing over here? And how come you let out that scream, Susan? You'd think something was after you! What's going on?"

"Tucky was afraid," Susan answered. "I brought him in here because he was afraid."

"Then he passed it on to you? Because one of those yips I heard certainly came out of you, Sue."

"I had a bad dream. And Tucky had one too."

Tucker withdrew to the other side of the bed. His lower lip protruded a little as he scowled at both of them.

"Not a bad dream! *They* came—*they* were right here!"

Susan saw Mike's mouth open, and she knew very well the question he was about to ask—one she did not want to hear, nor to have Tucker answer.

She shook her head at Mike and he give a slight nod. The many "dreams" of the past, which Tucker could summon up at will, were only too well known to both of them. Mike should be as eager as she not to get

101

Tucker started on another " 'maginary."

"But they went away, didn't they?" Mike asked matter-of-factly, as if some persons had passed him in the hall.

For a very long moment Tucker did not answer, and Susan felt a chill. She did not want these new inhabitants of Tucker's imagination to move in. There was fear, which there had never been before when Tucker announced that this or that had taken up living with the Whelans. Perhaps because, in the very ordinary house back at the Cape, the " 'maginaries" had been so impossible one could shrug them off, humoring Tucky. But here—here . . . She shivered.

"They don't go away—not all the way," Tucker said. "They have to wait. But they do that mostly in their own place."

"That isn't this room." Mike held the storm lamp a little higher, chasing shadows back to the far corners.

"No." To Susan's relief Tucker agreed. He also slipped down under the covers.

"Suppose you come in with me, Tuck. My bed's bigger than Susan's, and I promise you that I won't have any bad dreams—"

Susan was about to be sharp. Was Mike hinting she had put Tucker up to this? All right—let him take Tucky then.

She watched them out of the room without any protest. Suddenly she was very sleepy—just as if she had swallowed those pills Mother had to use for bad headaches, which made *her* sleepy. She just hoped she would not dream again.

The morning sun was steady through her windows

102

when she awoke again. Beyond her half-open door she could hear Tucker and Mike—at least the murmur of their voices from the bathroom. She pulled herself out of bed and went about the business of getting dressed—face and teeth to be cleaned as soon as the boys left the bathroom. It was her morning to see that Tucker's bed was made—since he was excused because of age from that particular chore, but *not* from keeping things tidy. Either Mike or she would inspect his room before they went downstairs. So she went over to Tucky's room now. It was plain that he had not returned to his own bed for sleep. The covers were turned down but no sheets had been twisted into untidy ropes, not had the pillows slid far over to one side or the other. It took her very little time to smooth it up for the day.

Then Tucker himself pounded in at his usual morning speed and she saw that Mike had combed his hair and seen that his T-shirt was not on back to front, which sometimes happened when Tucker, to whom clothes meant nothing, was thinking about something else.

"Hiya!" He greeted Susan. There was nothing remaining of that other Tucker—the one who had been so frightened the night before. Perhaps it had just been the storm, she decided. "Mike and me—we're going over to Johnny Fletcher's maybe tomorrow and see that good old dog."

Susan gave a sigh of relief and was even willing to listen to an endless tale concerning that "good old dog" when she came out of the bathroom, as Tucker again erupted from Mike's room, attaching himself to her, talking at near the top of his voice as she made her own bed, and, as Mrs. Kingsley put it, "neatened up" her room. He continued to talk all the way downstairs and into the kitchen.

"Miss Hendrika," Mrs. Kingsley announced as she put down bowls of oatmeal with a sprinkling of brown sugar across the top and brought out a basket of hot muffins, "said that you are to work in the library this morning. And you're to be good and sure you leave things in their right places. There's a gentleman coming to dinner tonight. He's real important, has something to do with a big library down state—one that buys the books Miss Hendrika writes. He wants to see some of the real old books that have always been in this house. So be sure you don't leave anything out of place where it can't be found."

Having delivered this order, she left them to eat and went on to deal with the wash. The current must have come on again in the night for they could hear the chug of the machine working away in what had once been called a summer kitchen. Though why there should be two kitchens in a house was a mystery to Susan. Surely the one they were in now was big enough to serve a family much larger than the Whelans and Great-Aunt—and Mrs. Kingsley, as well as Eloise.

Susan usually did not dawdle over breakfast, but today she chased bits of oatmeal around her bowl and made her second muffin last as long as she could by what was known to the Whelans as "mouse bites." She was very sure that Mike would not be turned from his purpose of continuing to trace down the "curse" by any uneasiness *she* might feel—nor any report of a bad dream in which paper dolls had come to life.

Tucker scowled. "Don't want to look at any old books!"

Before Susan or Mike could raise a hand to stop him, he had deliberately flipped a bit of oatmeal from a spoon straight at Josiah. The sticky stuff struck the big cat's chest and he jumped back from his dignified seat on the rag rug in front of the old fireplace. Luckily Mrs. Kingsley had her back turned, and a moment later Mike held his brother's wrist in a tight grip and pulled the spoon away from him.

Susan feared that Tucker might now enliven life by a tantrum. His bouncy feeling in early morning sometimes got out of control. Mike kept hold of his wrist and, when he got up, jerked his brother with him. For some reason Tucker did not at once return the attack by kicking out at Mike's shins. They got safely out of the kitchen and along to the library with no outbreak on Tucker's part. But he still looked angry and his face was beginning to flush in warning.

"See here," Mike said, once the door had closed behind them. Susan was looking around apprehensively at the glass cases and even the books. Tucker was prone to throw things when really aroused. "We are going to have a hunt, Tucker."

Susan bit her lip. Surely Mike as not going to break his promise and bring in the story of the curse again! He must not give Tucker any ideas!

"What kind of a hunt?"

Once inside the library Mike had loosed his hold and Tucker was free. He was not scowling any more, instead he watched Mike very closely, an odd look on his face.

"A hunt to learn things." At least Mike was not coming right out and saying what Susan hoped he would not mention. "You want to go over to Johnny's don't you?"

Tucker nodded.

"Well, you're not going if the G.-A. says no. She said there're rules here, and we've got to stick to them. The more we can show that we are doing that, the more pleased she's going to be. Then when we say we want to go to the Fletchers, she'll say—sure, go ahead. It works that way, Tucker, you have to learn that. You do what someone wants—they do what you want. It balances off, like those scales we saw at the auction. You put too much in one side and it goes down and won't straighten up until you even it off. Understand?"

Susan wondered just how far such reasoning would get with Tucker. Sometimes in the past it had worked. She crossed her fingers hoping that it would now.

"What things are we going to hunt? How can you hunt to learn?"

Tucker stood with his hands behind him, an obstinate look still on his face. "What . . . " He looked about now as if to find something that would provide a question Mike could *not* answer. "What about those?" He jerked a thumb at the beaded strips in the nearest case. "She said those were for reading—how do you read them?"

"We can find out. In fact, I've already found out a little. You go, Tuck, and look at those belts—that's what they called them—belts. Pick out one you want to know about and we'll find out what it means and surprise the G.-A. right out of her chair tonight, maybe when this

106

guy who knows so much will be here. How's that?"

Tucker actually looked impressed, turning at once to the case. Over his head Mike nodded at Susan and she understood that he had not forgotten their own project. Reluctantly, even more so since her dream, she went over to the section of children's books.

She had discovered Sunday that they were not in the same order as the books she had used in the school library—even though they were arranged in A's, B's, C's and so on by the authors' names. Instead, there was a short row of very old and dim-colored ones first. Then came two rows and a half of larger and less battered-looking ones, again running in an A B C pattern before a third section that filled three whole shelves, spreading into a fourth section that again spilled over onto another shelf. The big books on the wide bottom shelf seemed to be a mixture, along with the *St. Nicholases*, arranged in no real order at all.

Might as well start with the oldest books on the top shelf. Susan picked out a fat one. Any title on its back had long since worn away, and some loose pages tried to escape. She had to fit their brittle-edged bits back into the bindings again, afraid that the whole book might crumble into nothing in her hands.

The Fairchild Family. She looked at the title page first; then, very carefully, she turned to the inside of the cover. Yes, she saw something written there. She took it to the nearest window and held the book close to her eyes. The writing was all curly, as it had been on the backs of the dolls whose names she had first read, and part of it was the same:

"For Jethro, Emily, and Orrin from Mama. May

they enjoy this book as much as I did when dear Grandmother first read it to me, 1849."

Eighteen forty-nine, Susan must remember that. As she returned the book to the shelf, she stopped by the desk to get one of the tablets Great-Aunt Hendrika had earlier called to their attention. Susan wrote down the three names and the date. Of course nothing had been said about it being a birthday or Christmas gift, but perhaps Mike could figure it out when he got a chance. As she looked up, she saw that he and Tucker were still by the case. Mike had pencil and paper, too, and was copying a design from the belt onto the paper.

Now she picked a book from the second row: *The Story of a Bad Boy*. This was a taller one and the pages, though yellowed, did not seem as ready to fall out when she turned to the front.

"To Richard on his tenth birthday, 1878, from his sister, Bessie. Happy Birthday to a dear brother."

Susan scribbled those two names and that date—a birthday date—good. Mike could work back ten years from that easily enough, she thought.

The longest row of all was now before her. She dropped her hand onto a book with a red jacket, pulled it out, and turned to the front:

Horsemen of the Plains. The writing inside was a lot bolder and blacker.

"Merry Christmas, James. This is a bully story. Your friend, Ted—1914."

All right—she had three dates for Mike. Maybe she should make doubly sure and see if she could find some more birthday books. Susan was just considering the last row, trying to guess from their covers which might be birthday books, when she heard Tucker's raised voice.

"Then he would just say, 'Red belt,' and that could mean that they were going to fight?"

He was running fingers, probably still sticky from breakfast, along the front of the case, watching Mike, who was tall enough to look down into the case, not just through the side.

"Seems that was the way of it, Tuck. One lot of Indians—a tribe—would send a messenger with a lot of belts. He'd hold one up and make a long speech. Sometimes it was one about the past—how brave his people had been or something like that. Then they would all do a lot of talking back and forth before he'd bring out the belt with the real message—a red one for war, a white one for peace."

"How do you know?" Tucker demanded.

"I've been reading more of that old diary book ever since I found it, and it has a lot of stuff in it if you just keep reading. Jacobus Kuydall lived with the Indians for a while—he wrote a lot about them. But even he couldn't tell what all of these meant." Mike waved a hand over the lid of the case. "Some of the belts were very old, and people used them to remember what had happened a long, long time earlier. So after the tribes broke apart and the Indians who knew these stories died, no one was left to read the belts. These were used when the Revolutionary War came—you know—George Washington and all that . . .

"The Americans—they wanted the Indians not to fight on either side. They sent messengers with belts to talk about it with the Indians. There was an English-

109

man called Sir William Johnson—the Kuydalls knew him. He'd built a big house something like this one, and he was the man who talked with the Indians at the order of King George. He didn't want the Indians to fight either. But he was an old man and he wasn't very well. It was a hot day when all the Indian chiefs and their best warriors came to see him. They say that he talked most of the day and tried to keep the peace. And then it was just too much for him. He died that night.

"The men he had with him—they didn't believe in his way at all. So they told the Indians not to believe anything the Americans said—that they were lying and only trying to get rid of the Indians and take their land. The Indians—most of them—believed that, so they promised to fight for the British. Only one tribe, the Oneidas, would not agree. They tried to stay neutral, although some of their warriors later fought with the Americans . . . "

Susan had become so interested that she had joined the boys by the case of belts. Now as Mike paused for breath she said:

"The Kuydalls were part Oneida—"

"Yes. And some people said that it was Hendrik Kuydall who kept that tribe from going over to the English. That was what made his brother Jacobus and his father so mad at him when he went east to fight. Because they wanted the tribe to help the king. Both of them believed that the Americans did not have a chance, and that, when the king won, everyone who had fought against him would lose his land and even be put in jail or maybe hanged.

"So the Tories—those are the men who wanted to fight for the king—went up farther north and a lot of the Indians went with them. Then they started raiding down the valleys again—trying to take back the land. It was a bad time."

" 'Cause of the blue-eyed ones," Tucker said, to the complete surprise of his brother. "They were the worst ever, 'cause they were white men who dressed like Indians and did bad things, so the Indians would be blamed."

"Tucker," Susan demanded without thinking, "where did you hear about them?"

Tucker could not have read the torn-up book Mike had found as packing in her grab bag box. And Mike would not have told him.

"They were here," Tucker said shortly, then whirled away from both of them, heading for one of the windows. "Let's go out," he said, his voice a little shrill. "I'm tired of all this old stuff. And I don't like *them* . . . "

Mike looked at Susan and she could see that he was as surprised by that outburst as she was. Mike had certainly chosen the wrong thing to explain to Tucker. She supposed that somehow he had become so interested in it himself that he had forgotten a little about what had happened last night. Or perhaps, after Tucker had gone to sleep with Mike, he had not mentioned his reason for being afraid.

Mike had a pencil and paper, some of it already scribbled over with notes. He was also copying a design from one of the belts. Now he looked at the watch Dad had given him on his last birthday, nodded and shoved

111

his handful of penciled sheets into a desk drawer.

"Okay, Tuck. You coming, Sue?"

The outdoors looked clear and clean after last night's storm, far removed from that feeling of old, old things that clung so tightly to the house. Yes, she was ready. She put her own paper with its names and dates on top of Mike's. If he wanted to he could use that later. Right now she rather wished they could forget all the past Kuydalls and Kimbles of this too-old house. They were just Whelans and it meant nothing to them.

She saw that Tucker had a sweater, which he objected to, and then she got her own. Mike came out of his room. Under his arm he carried that big book from the library—the one that was the diary of Jacobus Kuydall. So he'd been studying the old diary in his room. No wonder he knew so much, Susan thought.

"Got to put this back, might just be something the G.-A. wants to trot out to show her tame professor or librarian, or whatever he is tonight."

"You had better stop calling her the G.-A.," Susan commented. "Someday you'll forget and do it to her face."

"D'you know—she might even like it." He grinned at her as he went down the stairs nearly two at a time, disappearing into the library to restore the diary. She wondered that he had dared take it away from there. Why Mike was so caught up in reading that old book she couldn't understand. It certainly was a long way from space ships and lunar probes, the things he had always read and talked about before. Maybe this house had changed him. She gave a small shiver. There were so many things she did not even want to think about.

Susan stopped in the lower hall, having sent Tucker on ahead, banging the door behind him. She looked into a dim old mirror hanging on the wall there. All the mirrors in this house were dim. They made people look misty, as if there were a fog floating around through the house.

Had she changed? No, she thought she looked the same. Her brown hair was, as Mother called it, "feathered," fitting itself neatly to her head. Her skin was very brown, though that would probably fade, she thought, with no hot Florida sun and beach to go to. She had a mouth that was a little too big and dark eyes and a nose a fraction too long. But she was still the very same Susan Whelan who had once lived in the south and now was not quite sure where she would live in the future. She only hoped it would not be here—for long.

Chapter

8

THEY WERE TO HAVE DINNER IN the dining room tonight—because Great-Aunt Hendrika's friend was coming. Susan was surprised and also concerned, because of Tucker, that they were going to share the event. It meant dressing up in Sunday clothes and remembering proper manners. Yet it appeared that Great-Aunt was determined for them to meet her guest and be "family," as if they were really Kuydalls. She had summoned them all in the afternoon to impress that upon them.

"Dr. Ferguson is one of the leading authorities on the history of this state. He is particularly interested in tracing some unusual material hinted at in the Voorman letters presented to the university only last year. The Voorman family is gone, old Captain Henry was the last, but he had the good sense to see that the family papers went to the university. So many people take no interest at all, and really priceless material is thrown out like trash!" She flushed when she said that. "I'll never forgive Hester for what she did in burning Hendrik's letters—and a Kimble diary, too! No, that is wrong of me! She never really understood the importance of that diary. And after her brother James's death when they were children, she developed such a strange aversion to everything connected with this house. It was really an obsession for a while. Then Grover—"

"Who was Grover?" It was Tucker who asked that— though Susan thought that Great-Aunt Hendrika had not really been talking to them but rather thinking aloud when she mentioned that name.

"Grover was Hester's son. He visited here in 19 . . . 1932." Great-Aunt Hendrika frowned. "He had had the flu pretty badly and Mrs. Elsie Kuydall invited him for a visit. Hester had to go to Texas with her husband. That was a hard time—not much money and Henry Kimble had lost his job and the trip to Texas was to see about a new one. He got it, too. Later they moved down there. But Grover was not as well as the doctors thought—he took a fresh cold and died here—" She ended abruptly. "Hester really hated this house after that, and when it was left jointly to us she would never come back at all. Just more silly superstition—of course! Now"—her tone became brisk—"you will be prompt for dinner. And I would advise you to listen. We are going to discuss some interesting things about local matters. Dr. Ferguson has agreed to take over the arrangements for the memorial sevice at the two hundredth anniversary of the raid. We shall dine at six—"

She made one of her abrupt swings down the hall, heading toward that other section of the house. Mike shrugged.

However, Susan was thinking of only part of what she had heard. James—who had died here. Could that be the James paper doll? And Hester, the girl in that family. What had happened to Orrin? She shivered. No, she really did *not* want to know. But at least there was no paper doll with the name Grover on its back. She was glad about that.

Tucker had gone into his room, but Mike stopped Susan. "Did you get those dates?"

"I got some. One is a birthday. The rest—I don't know whether they will mean anything or not."

Mike nodded toward Tucker's room. "Keep an eye on Tuck. I'm going down to see what I can find out."

He had left before she could protest. She looked in upon Tucker to find him sitting cross-legged on the floor, facing the picture-covered wall with a look of concentration on his face, almost as if he were watching TV. A house without TV simply bewildered Tucker. Susan had had a very queer thought that if there had been a TV in this particular house, it might have carried scenes she would not have wanted to see. Like a story Karen had told her—a scary one—about a little girl who saw bad things come right off a screen.

"It's a story . . . " Tucker startled his sister out of her thoughts. He was tracing with one finger on the wall at the level of his eyes.

Not about Indians, Susan hoped. She knelt to look. The pictures here must have been shielded from the full rays of the sun, for they were less faded, and they

116

had been put on with care and arranged in a line. There was a small boy wearing short pants and a loose shirt, who was having trouble with a kite. In the first picture he was carrying it under his arm (it was such a large one that its tail dragged on the ground) up on a hill. The second showed him running down the hill, the string in his hand, the kite now up in the sky. In the third, the kite was caught in the branches of a tree and there were some birds flying about in an excited way as if frightened. In the fourth, the boy was climbing the tree to get the kite down again. A dog appeared and was pulling at the loose kite string that dangled in the air.

The final picture showed the boy, with his head down, a torn kite in his hands, and the dog jumping about still with one end of the string in its mouth.

"He had to take it home and get it mended," Tucker said. "I bet his daddy could do that. It would be fun to have one of those—" He stabbed a finger straight into the kite. "How come we never had one?"

"I don't know," Susan admitted. Her attention slid away from the disastrous adventure of the kite to another set of pictures immediately above. Here there seemed to be another story—there were a girl and boy wearing very colorful clothes walking hand and hand into a woods. The girl had a basket in her other hand and the boy a branch of tree with all the leaves stripped off. Then they were on a path among the trees.

There was something very odd about those trees. When Susan looked closely they appeared to arrange themselves into faces—not nice faces at all. She blinked and blinked, and still the faces became more and more clear. In the third picture the two children had reached an open place in the wood where there was a strange littl house. She studied that with even greater attention. A gingerbread house?

The children—Hansel and Gretel? Susan remembered the puppet show they had done at school three years ago. Could be. But all those faces in the tree leaves? She examined them again. There was something familiar about them. First they looked a lot alike, even though they were in different places and made up of different kinds of leaves and branches. Susan shook her head determinedly. No. That could not be true! This was *not* the face she thought she had seen in the mirror last night, repeated over and over again! Was she getting like Tucky—seeing things that were not there and never could be?

Still later she was very glad—while she dressed in her new plaid dress and brushed her hair, trying to give it just the right swirl Mother had shown her— that the electric lights were working today. Outside it was getting dark. The mirror was no different from what it had been when she had inspected it that morning. She finished quickly to go back and make sure of Tucker, only to find Mike vigorously brushing his brother's hair.

"And don't open your mouth—" he was saying.

"Then I can't eat and I'm hungry." Tucker grinned and made a face at his brother. "I've got to open my mouth to eat."

"But not to talk. Remember—we want to even our side of the balance. You upset that and there won't be a visit to the Fletchers!"

"All right." Only Tucker was making another face, looking cross-eyed at his own nose, inserting fingers into each corner of his mouth to spread that wider.

"Aaachochee!" That sounded more like a sneeze than a word, but he had the attention of both Mike and Susan.

"What do you mean by that?" Mike wanted to know.

"Oh, she's the big one that dances with the two drums." Tucker was certainly not making sense. "There's the girl with all the cherries hanging on her like a dress—then Aaachochee. Only *she* can be mean when she wants to be—real mean!"

Susan signaled frantically to Mike. No more questions! They did not want to get Tucker started off on one of his flights of imagination right before they were to make a good impression on Great-Aunt's important Dr. Ferguson. Her brother was now staring at Tucker with a very queer look on his face, as if that babble *had* meant something to Mike.

She wanted very much to get Mike alone. Not only to ask about the results of his last visit to the library and whether the dates she had managed to find were of any help or must she try again, but because she realized that he *had* understood something about this Aaachochee-girl and also the one with cherries. There were far too many mysteries, and Susan felt she was being caught up in them as if she had blundered into a big, sticky, ugly spider web.

Only there was no time to ask. It was well known to both older Whelans that, no matter how Tucker might be reduced to order with clean face and hands, to leave him alone in that condition meant he would not remain so. Resolutely Susan took over while Mike went to finish his own preparations for a company dinner.

She was very tempted to ask Tucker a few questions herself, as they went downstairs, but knew the danger in trying that. So she chose the boring subject of the Fletchers' dog, which engaged him immediately, and tried to listen as he told her all the fine points about that animal and how he was going to get a dog just like him—as soon as he could show this canine marvel to Dad and find a similar puppy.

The library door was open. She heard voices inside and, without thinking, towed Tucker along.

All the lights were on and Great-Aunt Hendrika, wearing a full skirted dress which was almost sweeping the floor, her hair caught up in the back with a wide comb set with dark red stones, stood beside the same table of "belts" where Mike had earlier lectured them. Now the top had been raised and a man was reaching in to run his fingers along one of the exhibits.

"—fully authenticated," Great-Aunt said.

"But, of course! What treasures, Miss Kuydall! Even the Smithsonian cannot equal this! And all a part of your family history. You have records—ah, that is so fortunate. The tragedy is that some priceless things are simply tossed into the rubbish when our older families die out. I have heard of the most wanton destruction— enough to make any historian cringe. As you doubtless have yourself."

Great-Aunt Hendrika's smile had vanished. She gave a sharp nod.

"You will then think about offering your house as

120

one of the exhibits? A house tour here . . . " He raised his head to glance around the library, " . . . that would be an additional feature of interest, to many. There is Harnshaw—you know his life of Walter Butler—and Dr. Riberson, who has recently given a definitive lecture on the stand of the Six Nations during the war. With the present rising concern about racial roots, authentic Indian material is even more important. The Kuydalls themselves have Indian blood, do they not?"

"An Oneida ancestress in the direct line," Great-Aunt Hendrika answered him, but with no smile. She wore instead the shadow of a frown between her eyes. As if he were speaking about something she would rather not mention. Then, determined to bring it all into the open, she said abruptly: "I think you must also have heard that the Kuydalls were for a long time held in horror in this valley. Mistakenly for Hendrik, who was entirely innocent. But he and his descendents lived away from this house for nearly a century on that account."

"But my dear Miss Kuydall, that is a very old story. There are certainly no Tories now and the raids down these valleys are all just a matter of history. Even that so-called devil, Walter Butler, has found apologists among impartial historians and biographers these days. Your family being so divided in allegiance during the Revolution is no different from a number that I can list without even having to delve into records. Also, is it not true that those who participated in the raid here made the Kuydalls themselves suffer as much as nearly all the other valley people? The monument over in the church yard is witness to that. There is no shame attached in the least to *your* own branch of the family. Colonel Hendrik Kuydall was not responsible for his brother who, by all accounts, must have been demented. Was he not a man so trusted by Washington himself that he was offered a post in the new government once the General became President?"

"There were other things . . . " Great-Aunt Hendrika turned away from the case, having lowered the lid and turned a small key in the lock to one side. "I do not give any credence to superstition, Doctor, but a most unfortunate tale has clung to this house—and our family—ever since that raid. You have heard doubtless of haunted houses? It is the fashion now to write books and plays with as many horrors as the authors can cram in. A haunted house here—I would not like to have that story public property. I do not want to look out in the lane to see cars cruising slowly by while their occupants stare up at the windows here in search of some monstrous face."

"Monstrous face?" Dr. Ferguson looked bewildered. "But—"

"You have heard of the False Faces of the Long House?"

"Naturally. A secret society which, toward the end of the Iroquois era, is said to have become corrupt and used by certain sadists to further a quite bloody series of ceremonies. Though originally it was harmless and had something to do with fertility or harvest rites, I believe. There was a girl chosen to be the Cherry Maid, who led them in some of their ceremonies. But—"

"What had the False Faces to do with Kuydall affairs?" Great-Aunt Hendrika completed his unfinished question. "In the old days people would have told you that that secret society had quite a lot to do with us. No one knew its members. They appeared only masked, except for the Cherry Maid who was not really one of their fellowship. They were all considered to be sorcerers. Their drummers were said to be able to drum up either evil or good after blood was spilled and proper sacrifices made. As you yourself said, they became quite evil toward the end of their time. And they had a hand in Kuydall fortunes—according to family tradition. But that is another matter, and one I have no intention of explaining.

"As for a tour through the house—" She hesitated. "I would want to consider—"

"Even if you decided, as you have every right to do, against that, I trust, Miss Kuydall, that you will allow our committee a chance to visit and to explore."

"Explore?" Great-Aunt Hendrika looked surprised. "Explore where?"

It was Doctor Ferguson's turn to hesitate before he answered. He had a thick mat of gray hair covering his head and now he ran one hand through it and then scratched the neatly trimmed beard.

"This house is unique. Thomson wants to make a study of its architecture if you will allow. It was erected in the wilderness in the days when the usual shelter was the crudest of cabins or lean-tos. The plans for this house are closer to European design than they are to the city houses and estates of the coastal colonies. In fact, he would greatly like your permission to write a monograph on the subject. Perhaps you could also consider that . . . "

Susan had been too polite (or believed that she was being) to call attention to Tucker or herself. It was Tucker who broke into the conversation between the shaggy-headed man who spoke so quickly and so excitedly and Great-Aunt Hendrika. Susan had loosened her grip on him and he was out of reach before she could move, walking boldly up to Dr. Ferguson, placing his hand palm flat against the glass side of the Indian belt case, looking up at the man as he did so.

"These are books," he said. "Mike said that one"— he curled a finger to point—"meant they were going to fight in a war. But they didn't choose right. So they all had to go away when it was over. Only they didn't come here—" He was shaking his head. "They said 'no,' 'cause the people here were friends. It was those others . . . " He looked the same way he always did when he was trying to make some one else understand a thing he believed. " . . . they had blue-eyes—only they didn't—that was just a name which meant that they were bad men dressed up like Indians. And they were the ones—" He stopped short, his gaze shifting from the surprised-looking face of Dr. Ferguson to the case itself, as if he were trying to find a hiding place.

"Please . . . " Susan had hurried forward. "He's talking about the diary and the torn-up book. Mike was telling him a story about the belts and he gets things mixed-up at times. But it was in the book—the torn one from the grab box—all about how Jacobus Kuydall came back to rob the house and that the Indians wouldn't come. Only some other white men who wanted loot and dressed like them."

"Torn-up book—grab box!" Great-Aunt Hendrika

broke in to Susan's flurry of explanation. "What *are* you talking about, Susan?"

"The grab box I bought at the sale—with the dress patches—and"—she was a little hesitant as she added—"the paper dolls in it. You remember, Great-Aunt Hendrika. Somebody had torn up an old book and stuffed the pages in to pack the box tightly. Mike sorted out the pages and found a story about the raid—"

"Miss Kuydall!" Dr. Ferguson's voice sounded even more loud and excited. "Can it possibly be that this child is speaking of the Kimble pamphlet? If she is, such a discovery is priceless, priceless—"

"Mike has it?" Great-Aunt did not answer him, rather she asked Susan.

"Yes. He put it together. There were a lot of loose pages—really part of two books. But he put one together."

"Tucker"—Great-Aunt Hendrika turned to the boy—"will you run up and see if your brother is coming, and tell him to bring with him this paper book."

"The Kimble book—even if it is in loose pages—but all there . . . unbelieveable! Where did this come from, young lady? What is this grab box you keep mentioning?"

Before Susan could answer Great-Aunt Hendrika did it for her.

"My cousin, Hester Kuydall Kimble, died two months ago. She lived in the old Collins house. Since she had no direct heirs save me, and I was well endowed as she knew, she left the major part of her estate to the church. Some of the ladies cleaned out the attic and made up these cartons to be sold as grab

125

boxes—with the contents unknown. Susan invested in one—"

"Papers—were there other papers?"

Great-Aunt Hendrika wore her Commander face. "I regret to say that Hester did not see the value of anything to do with family history. She had the misfortune to lose her son when he was just a boy and was staying here. And her elder brother had died under this same roof when she was a child. She took a violent dislike to the house, really to anything that had to do with the past. It was only in her later years that she moved back to the valley, but she never came to this house, nor did she encourage any reference to earlier days.

"When my Aunt Elsie Sayer Kuydall died, Hester refused even to share in the estate. But some things were sent to her because they were especially mentioned in the will. I believe that she simply put them in the attic. If she had any other family papers, she carefully destroyed them before her death. I know of some that were so handled. We found nothing at all except a few concerning her own immediate family—"

"Yet the Kimble pamphlet . . . out of the attic . . ."

"We are not yet sure that is what it is," Great-Aunt Hendrika cautioned. "If so—I am surprised that Hester kept that."

Susan was not quite sure but she thought that when Great-Aunt Hendrika said "that" her voice had changed. Just then Mike came in, carrying the yellowed sheets, the edges curled or tattered.

"Come here, come here!" Dr. Ferguson called as if he did not see Mike at all, only what he was carrying. Already he had a hand out as if to snatch at the bundle of brittle paper. Then he gave a little laugh.

"Miss Kuydall—what you must think of me. I fear we all let our enthusiasms run away with us. I believe you are Michael Whelan, yes, and so a Kuydall, too, of another branch. If what you are holding there is what I suspect, you and your sister have indeed made a major discovery, one that will mean a great deal to our whole program. We have heard of the Kimble pamphlet. A very mutilated portion of it was found some years ago in an old desk being moved up in Utica. You see there was a legal battle over the publication of this piece of work.

"The Kasper Kimble who wrote it had a great dislike for the Kuydalls, even though they were distant cousins. It had been over a hundred years since the incidents he wrote about had occurred. Still, in some families, old feuds die hard. Apparently Kasper wanted to make his relatives squirm for some reason or another. Thus he wrote up the valley raid in the worst possible light, bringing back into common talk old hatreds and scandals of that time.

"Thadeus Kuydall bought up all the copies he could find, as well as taking the case to law as libel. He did not get far with that. However, the printer was frightened enough to sell him all the copies he had ready for sale. The plan had been to market it during the hundredth anniversary ceremonies of the valley massacre. So Kimble's plan to embarrass the Kuydalls failed and people forgot about it. But hints reached us through old diaries and letters that he made statements in it which had been purposefully suppressed by the family in later years, and that there was a whole different

127

tale to be told if one discovered the full truth of the matter.

"Now . . . " Once more he reached out as if to take the pages from Mike, and then shook his head slowly as if he must warn himself, looking beyond to Great-Aunt Hendrika. "I think that the final decision is up to you, Miss Kuydall. Your ancestor worked hard to suppress this. If it is the full text of the Kimble pamphlet, your niece and nephew here discovered it. So it remains a Kuydall decision as to what should be done with such a find." Yet he looked so eagerly at the papers Mike had that Susan half-expected something to happen as it did in magic stories—that the papers would pull themselves out from between Mike's fingers on their own and fly straight across to Dr. Ferguson.

Instead Great-Aunt Hendrika held out her hand and Mike surrendered the pages to her.

"This, too," she said slowly, "is something I must really think about."

Chapter
9

SUSAN HALF-EXPECTED DR. FERGUSON to ask again about the booklet, which Great-Aunt Hendrika put away in one of the drawers of the desk, one she unlocked—and locked again—with another small key such as she had used on the belt case. Instead he talked of other things through dinner, telling stories of his travels to locate material about the valley history. Some of his discoveries had been really exciting, though Susan would never have believed, before her own adventures here, that a search for old letters, or very badly-treated books and papers, could be a treasure hunt.

To her relief Tucker was quiet, eating his way through the meal without spilling anything. He also, as Mike had warned, kept his mouth shut when it came to talking. In fact he was so quiet that, after a while, Susan grew uneasy.

Tucker thinking, and she believed he was thinking, was to be watched. Another " 'maginary" might suddenly be added to their company. However, perhaps it was the Fletcher puppy that made him concentrate on his plate rather than the company.

After a while Dr. Ferguson began discussing with Great-Aunt Hendrika people who could be depended upon to serve on this committee or that—and whether they should try to expand the program this year. Susan blinked. She was not used to going to bed early, and she was well past the age of taking naps in the afternoon, but tonight she felt sleepy, and when she swallowed the water from her glass, or some of the blueberry pudding, her throat was scratchy, as if she had been talking a long time, or else was starting a cold.

At last they were excused, while Great-Aunt Hendrika and Dr. Ferguson returned to the library for coffee. Then Tucker roused from whatever daydream had held him during most of the meal.

"I want to see the Muppets," he announced.

"You know there's no TV," Mike answered tiredly as one who had said the same thing many times over.

"Why?" demanded Tucker.

"Because Great-Aunt Hendrika doesn't want one. You know that. So why keep on asking?"

Susan remembered the unpleasant idea that had occurred to her earlier—that perhaps TV in this house might be something very different.

"You've got a TV," she said.

"Huh?" Mike and Tucker stared at her.

"A different kind of one. You know, Tucker—you were watching it this afternoon—right on the wall of

130

your room—the boy with the kite and the dog?"

To Susan's relief Tucker nodded and made for the stairs.

"Got a TV—my own TV," he said, tramping hard on each step as he went, as if to impress that fact on anyone listening. Susan followed swiftly waiting for Mike. If the wall pictures could appease Tucker into thinking he did have a TV—that would solve one problem. At least he would not go banging into the library, demanding that the Muppets be shown on a screen that did not exist.

Mike followed them into Tucker's room while Susan switched on the lights. There was a lamp on the small table by the window, another on the bureau top. However, Tucker was already digging into a drawer to pull out the oversize flashlight that had been in his Christmas stocking, and which, for a while, had been one of his favorite possessions.

Now he squatted down on his heels—not in front of the boy and the kite story, which had drawn his attention that afternoon, but farther into the corner. What he beamed the light upon seemed at first to Susan to be part of a circus, and then she believed it was more like a visit to Disneyland.

A plump brown bear stood on its hind legs, not just standing but roller-skating, looking smug as if it thought it was very smart to be able to do such a trick. Beyond it were two monkeys wearing bright red jackets and small round hats. Each of them held a cord at the other end of which walked fat white ducks. Their wings were up, their bills wide open. They could be prisoners yelling for help.

131

Next came a camel with a big cat riding on its back as might a person. A big pink bow showed at the cat's neck, and in one paw it held a silly little pink umbrella. Beyond that was a huge mushroom. At least it was huge next to the little girl who stood by it, her hands linked behind her back, her head stretched up so she could see what sat curled on the mushroom—a very large green caterpillar, who wore a cap with tassels bobbing over one of its bulging eyes and held, in one of its many front feet, something on a cord, from the end of which came a small trail of smoke.

Tucker having settled himself at ease before this display glanced over his shoulder to his sister.

"What are they all doing?" he asked. Then waited as if he fully expected her to know a story that combined these queer animal people. Susan dropped down and gave a small gulp. Tucker was the one with the imagination. She had many times wondered how he could tell his tales and make them so real. She . . . oh, she had sometimes made up things to act out with Karen and Francie, but she never tried to equal Tucker.

"You know."

Tucker shook his head. "You don't know what the Muppets will do—not until you see them do it. These are Muppets—new Muppets—you said so. So . . . what do they do? Where did the bear get those roller skates and—"

"He bought them—just this afternoon." Mike knelt behind Susan. "He's practiced a lot on ones that belong to his brother, but it's his birthday. He got money and so he bought his own. He thinks he is going to be a champion skater."

Tucker looked from the bear to Mike and back again. "Will he be a champion?"

"If he practices hard enough," his brother replied firmly. "Those monkeys—they are bad. They have kidnapped the ducks, but they'd better watch out because when the bear catches up to them he'll make them let the ducks loose. Then the monkeys will have to run to get away."

"And the cat—she's in Egypt," Susan was suddenly inspired. "Remember those pictures Mrs. Robinson brought to show us. They went to Egypt last year and rode on camels to see the pyramids. Oh, and—the cat is hunting the temple where all the cats once lived. She wants to see where they were so famous in the old days." More of Mrs. Robinson's travel memories came flooding back. "It is very hot in the sun there. That is why she has that umbrella. But she thinks she is stylish, so she doesn't carry a regular umbrella but a pink one instead. And she wears a big ribbon bow. She is sure that everyone is noticing her!"

"And . . . " Now Tucker moved the light a fraction directing it on the caterpillar.

"That's Alice!" Susan was glad to meet a familiar friend, one she did know something about. "She's in Wonderland. There she drank something that made her very small—now she's asking that caterpillar how she can grow large again."

"Does he know?"

"Yes." Susan remembered this even better than Mrs. Robinson's Egyptian adventures. She had read *Alice in Wonderland* earlier that summer after her foot got infected when she stepped on something sharp on the beach. She had had to stay in bed a whole week. "She breaks off part of the mushroom and eats it; then she grows to her right size again! She has a whole lot of other adventures, too!"

Tucker studied the caterpillar and Alice. Then he gave a firm nod. "New Muppets. My own TV."

Susan leaned forward. There was another series of pictures above the animals Tucker had selected. Here were tiny men riding on grasshoppers, holding out spears that looked as if they might be made from pieces of grass. They were heading straight at each other as if they might be going to fight. Above them, in a bush with flowers and leaves, were tiny ladies, wearing dresses made from flower petals, who had long hair floating down their backs.

"And . . . " She pointed, fascinated by the ladies and the grasshopper riders. They must have a story too.

Tucker's hand swung up, pushing hers away.

"*My* TV!" he exploded. "Mine!"

Mike's hand was on Susan's shoulder. "All right— leave him to it. By the looks of this room"— she glanced up to see her brother looking from wall to wall—"he has enough to keep him looking for some time. Come on, we'll let him do his own storytelling."

Susan remembered Mike's quick trip to the library. She was willing enough to leave Tucker to his "New Muppets" and follow Mike to his room. He had spread out on the bed some note sheets and Susan settled down beside him.

"They were there, those names and dates in that old Bible. I didn't get a chance to check them all, but listen to this. Mike picked up the table sheet nearest to him

134

and began to read:
"Carolus Kuydall   1767
Johanna Kuydall   1769
Florian Kuydall   1774

"And after that was something in maybe Dutch. I couldn't read it—but the date was 1780."

Susan did some counting in her head. "They were eleven, thirteen, and six—just like us!"

"Yes, and that raid came in 1780. So I suppose that other stuff I couldn't read was about that. All right, here comes the next:
"Jethro Kimble   1838-1851
Emily Kimble   1840-1851
Orrin Kimble   1845-1865, killed serving his country"

"Two of them—thirteen and eleven—Jethro and Emily—but not Orrin," Susan said slowly.

"No, he was killed in the Civil War. Next:
"Richard Kimble   1867-1880
Bessie Kimble   1869-1914
Tod Kimble   1873-1880"

"Not Bessie, but the other two—that was a hundred years after the raid."

"I got the last one, too," Mike went on.
"James   1903-1916
Hester   1907—There was no other date for her.
She was the one who just died and nobody's put it in yet—that's what I think.
        "Orrin   1912-1942—he was killed in
                                    World War II."

"Grover?"

"Didn't have time to look him up. But that's the way it read." Mike smoothed out his paper.

135

"The first three—these are the ones no one knows what happend to. They're supposed to have been killed when they were being taken north for ransom. Then Jethro and Emily—they died together in 1851—just those dates. It doesn't tell why or how. In 1880 two more died—but not Bessie. And just one—James—in 1916. It really doesn't explain very much."

"Execpt that they all died here—or—near here," Susan said.

"Coincidence." Mike folded the paper. "That's all it is. This pamphlet, which that Kimble wrote, was what blew it all up into the curse business."

Susan was thinking of the dolls hidden at the bottom of her drawer. There was something—those families—always three—some with their faces made from parts of old photographs. Why had they been made in the first place?

"Tucker—" Susan began and then stopped. Tucky said a lot of things, but how much came from his " 'maginary" dreams and how much not, who could tell? Except she kept remembering what he had said about—*they*—waiting. She looked at the paper Mike had folded, half-expecting him to throw it into the wastebasket. Instead he tucked it into the front of the paper pad he had been using. Susan did not want to ask him why he was keeping it. She grabbed her own scribbled sheet and balled it up. Perhaps Dr. Ferguson would be interested in the paper dolls as a part of history. She thought about getting rid of them and it made her feel better. Yes, give them to him. He must still be here—she had not heard his car drive off and he must have a lot to talk over ith Great-Aunt Hendrika.

"Sure." She got up. "It doesn't mean anything!" Eagerly she accepted Mike's words, wanted to believe them true. It was only in this house that she thought about such things anyway. Back home—back home nobody ever worried about *old* things. And Mike—she looked at the row of books sitting on top of his bureau now. They were very dusty, the wording on their backs dulled so she could hardly make it out. Yet he had lined them up there as if he needed them. All his space books were in a topheavy pile on the floor.

"Did you get those out of your grab box?" Susan suddenly realized that she had never asked Mike what success he had had with his choice. She had been too interested in her own finds.

"Yes." He walked over and ran his hand along the old bindings. "There's a history of New York—and it ends in 1880! Here's a book about the building of the Erie Canal. There's another about the early settlers. Then these . . . " He pulled the last two out of line and flipped them open so that Susan could see pages that were covered, not with printing, but curlicued handwriting like what was in the big diary book that had caught Mike's attention from the first. "These are a couple more journals. This one's not too exciting. Seems to be from a store—buying this and selling that. But the other one was kept by a doctor, I think. Say . . . " He began to ruffle pages. "The date's right. There might just be something about the Kimbles—it says 1850 in the beginning—"

Susan was already at the door. "I don't want to know!" She did not look at Mike as she pushed into the hall. No, she did not want to know what happened to

Emily who had made the sampler picture still hanging on the wall, or to Jethro. They had nothing at all to do with her.

Back in her own bedroom, she sat down in the rocking chair to stare at the lower dresser drawer. For some reason she put both her hands between her knees and squeezed those tightly together. She did *not* want to look—to take out that box and look. Still another part of her did. She was being pulled one way and then another inside.

At last, against her will, Susan got up, opened the drawer, slid out the box and took it to the bed. She felt so queer inside that she kept swallowing, just as she did when car-riding too long, and the same shaming sickness was in her middle.

Her hands opened the box—bringing out James, Hester, Orrin. No, those were not the ones she wanted. Nor were Richard, Bessie, and Tod—Bessie and Hester . . . Was Hester truly the old, old lady who had just died? She tried not to pick up the next piece of cardboard; she did not want to see Jethro and Emily. Orrin somehow did not matter. He was one of the lucky one— Lucky ones? Susan shook her head as if to clear away some thought she hated. What did she mean by "lucky one"? Was there some difference in people— those people the dolls were meant to represent—so that the curse worked only against *them*? That was a queer idea which stuck in Susan's head. Tucky—he *was* different. She shivered. Had Jethro and Emily been like him?

They were real, far too real—with their faces, which were not just made-up doll ones, but faces that must

138

have once looked into the dim mirrors in this very house. Only maybe then the mirrors had been brighter. She slid Orrin back and put Emily and Jethro together before her. This had been Emily's own room once, Susan was sure of that. She shivered. To live in a house where so many, many people had come and gone—people about whom there were queer stories—it was frightening.

Her hand hovered now above the last cardboard divider in the box. Those others—the three faceless ones. Those . . . yes, she would certainly give them to Dr. Ferguson. And she was not going to look at them! Nothing could make her do it!

Hastily she replaced the dolls. She would give him these tonight, send Emily out of this room so Susan could forget her. Tomorrow she might even take down Emily's sampler and put it away. She did not want to remember Emily at all.

Susan had them repacked in the box and was down the hall at the top of the stairs when she saw Dr. Ferguson standing by the front door saying good night to Great-Aunt Hendrika. Before she could call out, he was gone, leaving her holding the box, still wanting to be rid of it and all it held.

Slowly she returned to her room. From Tucker's room came the murmur of voices. It was Mike's turn to oversee bedtime for the youngest Whelan. Susan closed her door and rammed the box back in the drawer, slamming it shut. She looked around. There were those books on the top of the stand, she had inspected them days earlier. Like the ones on the shelves downstairs, she had found them strange. Now she picked up the one at the end of the line.

Almost fearfully, she opened it to the front page. Yes, there was a name there: "Hester Kuydall." *The Princess and Curdie.* There was a picture opposite the title page of a lady wearing a flowing dress of green, with a green jeweled crown on her head and, facing her, a boy and a man. Hester's book. Susan was not afraid of Hester's book.

She got ready for bed quickly, adjusted her lamp for reading. Luckily Great-Aunt Hendrika had never given any orders that books could not be enjoyed in bed. Then she opened the book.

" 'Curdie was the son of Peter a miner' . . . " Good! Nothing to do with old houses, curses, or Indians, blue-eyed or otherwise. Susan determined to get into Curdie's world where she was sure such things had never been known.

She grew sleepy at last, but she had been thoroughly lost in the story. Paper dolls were far from her mind as she switched off her lamp and settled down. No storm tonight. Instead a full moon shone into the room, driving shadows back into the corners.

Susan suddenly pressed her hands to her middle. She was afraid. There was something in this room, something—someone—*someones*. She could not see them, but they were there. With them came this fear that made her sick and dizzy. She must get away. Not from them—no. They were as afraid as she was—she knew that they wanted her to be safe with them—to be away from what was coming . . . It was dark, and bad—very bad!

They were shadows. Still within the shadow, parts

of them were visible—faces and hands. Susan was not sure of the faces, but the hands reached out for hers, to help her, to take her where it would be safe. She was so afraid!

"Come!" She was not sure that she really heard that voice. Had someone actually called her? Or was it somehow just in her head? Susan could not tell what was happening to her. But the fear was making her sick, and those hands were reaching for her. They would touch her soon; then she would have to go with them. She *must* go with them. That was the only way to be safe!

"Susan!"

She was swaying back and forth. Had the hands caught hold of her? Were they pulling her out of bed—to go with them?

"Susan!"

The sharpness of that voice broke her dream. There were no shadows waiting. The light in the room was no longer moonlight. The hands on her shoulders were Mike's, shaking her vigorously.

"Wake up!" It was not Mike's everyday voice ordering her to do that, but one that kept the fear alive in her. "Tucker's gone!"

"Gone?" Susan had been so caught in her fearful dream that she was still in a fog. "Tucker?"

"Yes, Tucker!" Mike sounded angry. "What's the matter with you? I couldn't get you to wake up. Come on—we've got to find him!"

Susan was shaking so she could hardly slide out of bed and get her robe, huddling it about her shoulders as she stuck her feet into her bedraggled old scuffs. The bare floor beyond the carpet strips was cold. In fact the whole room was so chilly that she shook and shook.

"Where could he go?" She had a hard time thinking, as if her mind was all mixed up. Almost she expected to see hands still reaching for her.

"I think he went downstairs somewhere," Mike answered. "I heard that step near the bottom creak. But by the time I looked there was no one there. Remember when he used to walk in his sleep? Before they took him to Dr. Ramish back home?"

"Yes." Susan was finally alert enough to understand. "He can't get outside, can he?"

"I don't think so. Those doors have bolts on them—mostly too high for him to reach. Come on!"

"Great-Aunt—Mrs. Kingsley—" Susan scrambled after him. Mike had not turned on the hall lights. He had Tucker's big flash in his hand instead and was sending its beam toward the head of the stairs.

"Mrs. Kingsley's clear across the yard—remember?" he snapped at her. "And Great-Aunt is in the other wing. Come on—we're wasting time!"

They plunged down the stairs. Mike paused at each room to shine the light in a big circle about it, the drawing room with its plant room opening off it in the tower, the library, the dining room. At last they headed on into the big kitchen.

Susan caught at Mike's sleeve, so that the light from the torch danced in a flighty pattern across the huge room. The door to the cellar stood wide open, something Susan knew was not right. Mrs. Kingsley always kept it closed and put the heavy bar across it.

Just before that open door crouched both Josiah and

142

Erasmus. The ears of the cats were flattened against their skulls, while the ridge hair along their spines stood up, and their tails, fully bushed, swung back and forth. Though Josiah's mouth was open, he made no sound. A continuous growl came from Erasmus. They might almost be warning something off, as they stared downward into what was complete darkness.

"But . . . Tucky would not go there!" Susan protested. Tucker, after he had left the cellar the first day, when they had helped clear out the old storeroom, had always pretended that even the door to the stairs did not exist. Susan had seen him circle out and around so that when he came to the breakfast table he would not have to even go near it. Tucker would *not* have ventured into that place in the dark of the night. There was no sign of light below.

It was Erasmus who, with a last growl, flowed, belly down, onto the dark of the stairs they could not see. Josiah, after another silent protest—or challenge—followed. Mike shook his head.

"He must have gone there."

"I don't believe it!" Still Susan was with Mike as he crossed the room to shine the light downstairs. The rank, musty smell seemed stronger and nastier. Now the light caught the cats' eyes so that four glittering balls were upturned in the direction of the children before they disappeared.

"Tuck—" Susan had gotten out only part of the call when Mike caught her fiercely by the arm.

"Don't wake him if he's down there!" he ordered.

She gulped as she remembered. Tucker had been steered back to bed before, led back without waking at

143

all. What if he was shaken out of sleep, to find himself in a place of which he was frightened?

Mike started down the stairs and Susan followed. That sick feeling that had been a part of her dream was again rising in her. She swallowed and swallowed, holding on to the stair rail so tightly her nails dug into the old wood.

Chapter
10

IT WAS SO COLD. DIMLY SUSAN REAL-ized the cold was inside her. She had to force herself to take one step and then another. This was not part of the dream of the reaching hands. No—she was awake. Still, she was caught by the same fear. She grabbed at a fold of Mike's robe, held onto it, breathing in gasps.

The door to the fruit closet was closed, but the one to the dank and bad-smelling room where Mike and Susan had gone for baskets was open. Josiah crouched there, his tail switching, a low growl coming from his throat. There was no sign of Erasmus.

There was another sound as well, a pounding, and, through that, a whispering, so low Susan could not make out the words. Mike shoved past Josiah, who spat and aimed a fast-striking paw at him. Mike yelped as his pajama leg tore.

Susan loosed her hold on her brother. She had always been just a little afraid of both the large cats. This time she was more afraid of what was closing about them, of what waited around them. If she closed her eyes, if Mike left her—what would she see—or *feel*!

There were still piles of baskets fitted into one another, cartons pushed against one wall. To the right Mike's circle of light caught and held Tucker in its full beam.

The younger boy was on his knees, his fists pounding against the stone wall. His eyes were closed, but his mouth was open and from him came that whispering, not words—rather a whining sound.

Mike thrust the torch toward Susan and she took it, trying to keep it centered on Tucker. Back and forth behind the small boy paced Erasmus, his ears flattened, his back arched, his tail puffed, lips pulled back to show his teeth, though he was not growling. He did not seem angry with Tucker. At least he did not strike out at the little boy as Josiah had done at Mike, rather he was watching the wall against which Tucker was pounding.

Mike drew a deep breath and stooped to put his hands on Tucker's shoulders. The smaller boy twisted, fighting against that hold. His crying changed into words at last:

"Out . . . out . . . out . . . !" The three words became a scream. Then, so suddenly that he almost slipped out of Mike's hold entirely, he went limp. Mike fell to his knees, pulled down by Tucker's weight.

Tucker's hands, bruised, with spots of blood on the knuckles, lay limp and unmoving. His mouth was slack, drooling at the corner. His eyes remained tightly closed and he showed no sign of being aware of where he was or that Mike now held him. Susan stood over them, beaming the torch downward. That terrible choking in her throat grew worse. She raised her other hand and pulled at the collar of her robe.

"He's still asleep. We have to get him back," Mike said.

Could they, Susan wondered? Mike was strong, but Tucker was no lightweight and there were those steep stairs.

"Take the torch, brace it to shine down the stairs— No, what's the matter with me? Just turn on those lights Mrs. Kingsley used. It may take us both to get him up."

It was as if she had to wade through something thick, anchoring her feet fast. Gasping and fighting against what she could not see but that tried to hold her, Susan went, hating to take the flashlight, to leave Mike and Tucker together in that awful place, but knowing she must have light herself to find the switch.

The frightening heaviness about her did not lift. She had to pull herself up step by step to where she could push the switch. Light came—making her blink. The steps were bare, there was nothing on the floor. Whatever had tried to hold her was gone with the dark. Josiah no longer sat in the open doorway to the basket room, nor did he show any signs of anger when she passed him outside it.

There was light in the basket room, too. Mike had somehow gotten Tucker across his shoulder as Susan had seen people being carried away from fires on TV. She hurried to help so that when they started back up

147

the stairs she was behind, her hands out to steady Tucker's body where she could to take the strain off Mike.

Back in the kitchen she hurried once more to turn on lights while Mike lowered his brother into the rocking chair Mrs. Kingsley kept by the window. Tucker moved his head against the pillowed back and moaned.

Susan hurried to tear loose a handful of paper towels, held them under the cold water tap and then returned and patted the backs of Tucker's hands. They were bloody, and the skin was torn. He must have beat hard upon the old stones for some time.

"First aid kit . . . " Mike took the torch from the pocket of Susan's robe to disappear toward the front of the house. She wanted to bar the cellar door—but the cats had not followed them up yet, and she was sure that she dared not leave them shut down there.

Gently she brushed back Tucker's hair. His face was so hot! He continued to moan as if something hurt him—maybe his hands, and perhaps she had been too quick to try to wash them. Or maybe Tucker was sick!

Susan sat back on her heels, twisting the wet towels until they were a soggy mess and the whole front of her robe and nightgown were wet, clear through to her skin. Tucker—sick—like Emily, and James, and . . .

Mother—Dad! She wanted them! She wanted to be home again safe. There must be a doctor—Great-Aunt Hendrika would know. Thoughts sped through her head very fast, none staying long enough to be any help.

"Here!" Mike nearly skidded on the well-scrubbed floor of the kitchen, the first aid kit in his hands. He had the lid up and was busy bringing out bandages while Susan, whose fingers shook, dropped her wads of wet paper and tore open the packets he found. Tucker's eyes opened and he cried out.

"No! That hurts!"

He tried to pull away from Mike, but Susan held fast to one hand while her brother made a good job of covering up the raw and bleeding skin. Tucker freed the hand that Susan held and hit her hard with it.

"It hurts!" he cried looking straight at the two of them as if he did not really see them, Susan thought. She could not even be sure that Tucker was truly awake.

"Michael, Susan! Just what is going on here!"

Great-Aunt Hendrika came into the kitchen staring at the three of them in open amazement.

"Tucky—he walked in his sleep," Susan answered as she caught at Tucker's other hand, holding it fast for Mike to bandage. "He used to do this—a long time ago."

Tucker twisted and began to really fight, kicking out at his brother and sister, squirming as if to get out of the chair. Susan had to give her full attention to holding him, so Mike could finish bandaging the other fist. "What happened to his hands? Here, Susan, let me hold him. How in the world did he get those nasty bruises? Falling?"

"He was down in the cellar." Mike made tight the last strip of tape. "We found him hitting the wall there—in the dark . . . "

Great-Aunt Hendrika knelt by Tucker, tried to hold him still.

"Tucker! Why he's burning up—fever . . . " Her voice sounded queer. She was staring at Tucker as if she saw something just as frightening as those shadows in Susan's horrible dream. "Come on—we must get him to bed. Call Dr. Phillips . . . "

As she loosed her hold and Mike drew away to close up the aid kit, Tucker moved. He wriggled free and, though Susan made a hurried grab, he passed her, heading again for the open cellar door. It was only when Mike threw himself forward to catch his brother around the waist, holding him, in spite of Tucker's kicks and frantic struggles for freedom, that he was stopped from bolting back into the dark.

His face was very red now, and he was making funny noises that sounded like the deep growls of Josiah. Susan was convinced that this was not just Tucker in one of his tempers, that he did not really know what he was doing. There was something very wrong with her brother, a part of all the wrongness that had closed about her in the dream.

There was a streak of black and then of particolored fur up the stairs, as the cats at last erupted into the kitchen. Susan ran past Tucker, still fighting frantically in Mike's arms, to slam the door. She grabbed at the bar and dropped it into place. She had a feeling that she had shut out only a part of what was wrong, that a darkness still shadowed them all.

Mike could not try to carry Tucker while he was fighting. It took Great-Aunt Hendrika and Mike together to force the small boy away from the cellar door. He was on his feet now, seeming to have strength beyond what any one person could control. But they got him back down the hall and pulled him upstairs step by step. Tucker fought all the way. Twice he actually leaned over and bit at Mike's hands. Susan's early fears were swallowed up in a terrible new one. She had never seen Tucker act this crazy in all his tempers.

Somehow they got him into the upper hall, though now he threw himself down as a limp weight. Mike and Great-Aunt Hendrika had to lift him between them, while he continually moaned and then shrieked.

"Out—out of the dark!" Yet Susan had run ahead to turn on every light and the dark was gone.

When they at last got him back in his room Tucker gave a last scream. Susan shrank against the wall. As he cried out, his body stiffened. When they lifted him onto the bed he lay there unmoving. Only his eyes were open, staring up at the ceiling.

"Susan." Great-Aunt Hendrika's voice trembled, her face looked very pale and for the first time really old. "Go and get Mrs. Kingsley. Turn on the outside lights— the switch is by the back door. There is a bell right under the switch. Press that and keep on pressing it until you see the lights go on in the carriage house. She will come as soon as she can. That is our agreed upon signal for help. Then—go to my room and get the small directory by my phone . . . "

Susan sped out of the door, glad—and rather ashamed for being glad at the same time—that she did not have to watch Tucker now. She hated to go back to the kitchen, but she ran to find the switch and then the bell below, planting her thumb fast upon it.

Would those lights she had been told to watch for

151

never answer? At last there was a bright burst from the carriage house window. She flew upstairs and into the other wing of the house. Great-Aunt Hendrika had left a light on in her bedroom so it was easy to find the silk-covered notebook beside her phone. Grabbing it up, Susan started back.

Mrs. Kingsley was coming up the stairs, a plaid robe showing beneath the hem of her usual black coat.

"What's the matter?"

"Tucky's—Tucky's sick!" Susan answered, as she ran down the hall.

There were no sounds from her brother's room, no more screams—none of the strange moaning. As she burst in she saw that he was still stretched stiff on the bed, a quilt over him. Mike stood staring at Tucker's set face.

Notebook in hand Susan joined her brother. "Mike— he's never been like this before," she said. "Why—?"

"I don't know!" he snapped, never taking his eyes from Tucker. "We've got to call Dad and Mom . . . "

Susan swallowed twice, her throat hurt, and that feeling of not being able to breathe fully was back. Mike—Mike was afraid!

Great-Aunt Hendrika had her hand on Tucker's forehead as Mrs. Kingsley came in.

"The thermometer, Martha. I will try to get Walter Phillips. This is one time when a house call is necessary."

"Mom and Dad—" Mike raised his voice. "We have to call them!"

Great-Aunt Hendrika did not look in their direction but she nodded.

"We shall. But we'll get Walter first, middle of the night or no middle of the night." Her face was set. "Can you watch him until Mrs. Kingsley gets back?"

"Yes." Mike's jaw shot forward a little, as if he wanted to take care of Tucky by himself. Susan only hoped that Tucky would not again become fighting mad and try to get away.

They could hear Great-Aunt Hendrika on her way down the stairs toward the hall phone.

"Mike, what is the matter—please . . . " Susan reached out her hand to him.

Before he could answer Tucker moved for the first time since they had put him on his bed. He raised his bandaged hands to his face and began to cry. Not with the angry gasps he used when he was hurt or wanted something—but like someone who was alone and very frightened.

At that same moment Susan felt a sick swirling as if the room—the light—everything—was whirling around and around. She was caught up in a fear so great that she was not Susan Whelan any more. There was no safe place, only a dreadful dark holding her forever and ever . . .

There was a hand in hers and then she reached to find another. She had closed her eyes because the sickness made her so weak she could not stand. She was sitting—partly lying—and she was holding two hands, one smaller and one larger. The hands were real, holding off the terrible dark and the fear. Yet there was no comfort from them—only still she must hold them.

"Carolus, Florry . . . " Names and hands, those matched. They were all in the dark together. There

153

would never be any light anymore . . . "Carolus! Florry!" Her fear was icy cold and she was being swallowed by the dark—"*No!*" There was something else—something that fought the dark, that made her force her eyes open.

She was partly on a bed, and there was light here. "Florry?"

No—this was Tucker! His face had turned toward hers and his eyes were on her.

"Hanny?" He spoke in a voice hardly above a whisper. "We got out—we did, Hanny!"

"Tucker! Susan!"

Susan did not want to answer—though why Tucker should call her by that strange name she could not understand. She held one of his bandaged hands and her other arm was stretched across his body so that her fingers gripped, with a hold tight enough to be painful, Mike's fist.

Mike looked at her with the same strange fear that had been in his face earlier when he had watched Tucker.

"Tucker!" He said urgently. "Tucker!"

Tucker's head swung away from Susan to look toward Mike. Susan loosed her hold on the older boy's hand. That awful feeling of the dark and being swallowed up was gone. She was no longer dizzy. But some of the strangeness of those moments still held her.

"Carl . . . we got out!" came Tucker's half whisper. Susan sensed that he, too, had been caught in the same terrible dark. Only why did he call Mike by that other name?

A small frown began to show on Tucker's face. He

154

closed his eyes and then opened them again, slowly.

"You—you are different—" he said, almost in a complaining tone. "You have another face—only it ain't a painted one. Take it off—please, Carl, take it off!" His words grew more hurried as he lifted himself a little, waving one of his bandaged hands toward his brother's face as if to dislodge a mask which certainly was not there.

"Tucker . . . " Mike gently pushed him flat again. "Listen—you are Tucker—I'm Mike—and that is Susan." He nodded to her across his brother's body.

"Tucker, Mike, Susan—" Tucker repeated those names first as if he did not know them at all, and then a second time. "I'm Tucker—I am!" There was more force than a half-whisper in that cry. "I'm not there—I'm not *there!*"

Susan sighed, weak with relief. This *was* Tucky, the Tucky she had known and who had somehow been lost. Had he also been caught in that same dreadful place of dark that had come out of a dream to torment her?

"You're Tucker," she said, "I am Susan, and that is Mike. We're all together. Oh, Tucky—I'm so glad!"

"*They're* together, too." Tucker's face clouded over again. "Only—I can't just remember—and I should— I should—!" He pounded his free fist on the bed. "Make me remember, please, Susan, make me remember!"

"Susan, Mike, please come away from your brother. I want to take his temperature." Mrs. Kingsley had shed the coat she had worn earlier. Now she was waving a thermometer in one hand. "Open your mouth— there—under the tongue . . . Now." She had taken

Tucker's wrist out of Susan's hold, neatly elbowing Susan away from her perch on the bed.

Susan had half-expected her brother to resist. In the past, Tucky had never taken well to being sick. However, he lay quiet, the end of the thermometer pointing up from between his lips, the frown back on his forehead. She sensed that Tucker was trying somehow to remember. And she was sure that would be the worst thing in the world for him. But given Tucker's usual determination she did not know how he could be stopped.

Dr. Phillips appeared some fifteen minutes later, and shooing out everyone but Mrs. Kingsley (whom he greeted as if she were a trusted assistant), he took over and eventually stated that Tucker was to do no more remembering that night.

He fronted Great-Aunt Hendrika, Mike and Susan in Susan's room across the hall. He looked at the three of them as if he did not know quite how to begin.

"How is he, doctor?" Great-Aunt Hendrika demanded.

"There is a low degree of fever. But my guess is that the boy has had some kind of shock. I understand that he has sleepwalked before?" He looked to Mike.

"Yes, after the accident. You see he was going to nursery school about two years ago and there was a car smash. Tucky wasn't hurt more than getting his arm bruised and a bump on his head. He was in the hospital about a week however, because the doctor said there might be concussion. But the x-rays were okay. He slept a lot afterwards and once in a while he sleepwalked. But then he went to Dr. Ramish and it gradually

156

stopped. The doctor said it would."

"I see. Now what happened tonight? It is very apparent this boy has had a very bad experience . . . "

Susan and Mike locked eyes. The truth sounded (at least Susan thought it would) completely crazy. Yet they could not tell it any differently. However, because of her dream—that dream which seemed so much a part of it—she would let Mike tell it.

"Tucker—well, Tucker has a very vivid imagination. And he found out some stories about this house . . . "

The doctor glanced at Great-Aunt Hendrika. She was frowning.

"The funny thing is that he hates the cellar and will not go down there at all. Tonight he went to sleep all right. But Susan and I, we've been taking turns checking on him because he has had a couple of nightmares. I was reading and then I thought I'd better see how he was doing . . . "

At least, Susan thought gratefully, Mike was not going to bring in her nightmare.

"He was gone. So I thought maybe he was sleepwalking again. I got Susan and a flashlight and we went to look for him. It was queer, because Tucker doesn't like the house and I couldn't believe he'd go roaming around by himself."

With straightforward detail Mike told all the story—of their finding the cellar door open, of going down to find Tucker beating on the wall of the storage room and of how they got him up to the kitchen where Great-Aunt Hendrika found them.

"That's how he got those cuts on his hands. I know some first aid and I fixed them up. Then we brought him up to his room—"

"He came with you—he was awake by then?"

"He seemed awake, but he was fighting to get back to the cellar," Mike admitted. "It must have been some kind of a dream."

"Did he say anything?"

"Just 'out—out—' " Mike continued truthfully. But he did not mention the names Tucker had called them, or that bit about him supposedly wearing a mask.

"Where are the boy's parents?" Dr. Phillips asked.

"In Utica; I intend to call them."

"Perhaps it would be well. Physically, except for those bruised hands, he's in good shape. But I would certainly recommended some sort of counseling. He is plainly coming out of a state of fear of some sort, and with his history, this is a matter that must be taken care of. There is a slight degree of fever—but no cause I can see for that—it may be entirely emotional. I would advise that he not be left alone. Mrs. Kingsley has had excellent training—let her look after him for a while. And by all means keep an eye on him.

"At the present he appears completely awake and aware of where he is—but . . . " He shook his head, "There is always a reason behind such manifestations as this sleepwalking. You"—he turned to Mike and there was a harder note in his voice—"haven't been telling him any stories that would excite him, have you?"

Mike flushed and Susan was hot with indignation. "Mike doesn't do things like that! We know about Tucker. He has always imagined things and he didn't want to come here at all. Ever since he's been here he's been making up things!"

The doctor shrugged and Great-Aunt Hendrika made a little motion with her head. He nodded and they went out together. After a moment or two Mike and Susan could hear the murmur of voices from the lower hall.

Chapter

11

MIKE, THOSE NAMES HE SAID—HANNY, Carl—" Susan steadied herself with one hand on the tall foot of the old bed. "And wanting out." She sucked in a deep breath before she went on: "Mike, there was a dark place and I was holding on to someone, too—two different someones—and we couldn't get out!"

She fully expected Mike to tell her she had been dreaming, or else imagining things just the way Tucker did. Instead he stood there frowning—though she did not believe that he was mad at her for what she had said.

"Why did he pound on that wall?" Mike asked slowly, not expecting any answer from her, she was sure. "Carl—Hanny—" He repeated the names. Then he thudded one fist against the footboard of the bed with the same force Tucker had used in beating against the

160

old stones below. "What's the matter with—with all of us?"

Susan swallowed, ran her tongue tip across her lower lip as she often did when she was in a car and trying not to think of being sick. Because she felt now the same old churning in her stomach.

"*They*—they were here. They wanted me to come—they were so afraid—" She was talking a little wildly. Again it seemed that, though the light was now on in her room, those shadows were gathering right behind Mike, between her brother and the door, and that very soon hands would reach out beckoning, perhaps even pulling—Mike? Her?

"Who?" Mike demanded sharply.

Susan shook her head. "I thought it was all a dream. Maybe—maybe it wasn't after all. Maybe . . . "

Certainly it was against her will that her head turned—just as if someone had put two hands, one on either side, above her ears to force her eyes toward the bureau. In spite of her struggle not to move she took one step and then another in that direction.

Mike did nothing to stop her. She suddenly was not even aware he was there except as a shadow not nearly as important as the other presences now growing stronger all the time. They had called Tucker. Susan had a flash of understanding as she stooped to draw open the bottom drawer. Now they were using her—in a different way.

She took out the box of paper dolls and brought it back to the tumbled covers on the bed. With one hand she smoothed the covers as she opened the box with the other. Hurry—hurry . . . She upended the box, using

161

none of the care she had when she had unpacked her find.

Dresses, dolls fluttered down. They fell so oddly—not all together in one pile—but rather as if something in the air sorted them out even as they fell, the top ones now on the bottom.

James, his serious face uppermost, James—as if Mike's voice repeated his discovery from the old Bible—1903-1916. He lay to one side, while Hester and Orrin Two fluttered away with their clothes to a little distance.

Then came Richard and Tod—right on top of James. But Bessie—she made a side landing apart from her brothers.

Jethro and Emily, somehow Susan was not in the least surprised to see them join Richard, Tod, and James. While Orrin the First went down on the growing pile of clothes and seemingly discarded dolls. It was the first pile that was the important one. Those others did not matter. Jethro and Emily, both dying in 1851.

The last piece of dividing cardboard stuck. Susan had to use her fingernails to loosen it in the box. She did not want to, she did not want in the least to see Johanna, Carolus, and Florian. Yet she had no control over her fingers picking hastily at the obstruction, freeing the three last dolls, the faceless ones. They landed across Jethro and Emily, their heavier and slightly larger bodies covering most of that pile of dolls.

Susan threw the box from her and stood staring at the dolls. There—there were faces coming. No! She was

162

not going to look—she wouldn't! However, just as that force she had not understood had made her bring out the box, so now she could neither turn away her head nor close her eyes.

"Johanna, Carolus, Florian—" She heard herself repeat the names aloud as if she were calling them. No, she mustn't do that! That was what had happened before—always it had happened before! There had been Emily and Jethro, and then Richard and Tod, and James . . . and maybe even others, who had not been afterwards remembered by dolls.

"I—I won't—" Susan's mouth felt stiff and queer as she forced out those words. "I won't—and—" She grew more frightened, though she also felt angry as well. "Tucky—he won't either! You can't make him. He isn't going to go with you! He isn't!"

She knew as well as if she had read it in that diary Mike had found or in the torn-up pamphlet, what had happened to Tucker, what they were trying to make happen to her. They wanted—out! They called, but when someone tried to help them—then—then . . . Susan cringed away from the bed. No, it was not going to happen to Tucky! Nor her, nor Mike!

"Susan!"

There was a hurting hold on both her shoulders, her head flopped back and forth. Then came a sharp slap across her face which made her gasp with pain. She saw Mike between her and the bed on which lay the dolls—those dolls who could call—and call—

"Susan, what is the matter?"

Her mouth worked, she could feel it shaping words,

but somehow she could not hear herself saying them. Then she made a great effort and produced a small croak of sound which at last might be heard.

"It's *them*." She raised her arm with great effort, and though Mike was now between her and the bed, she pointed in the direction of the dolls. "It's Johanna, and Carolus and Florian. They call—they want—Tucky—Tucky—maybe me! They called James, and Richard, and Tod, and Emily and Jethro, and they died, all of them. Now they want— But they aren't going to get Tucky!"

She gave a sudden twist with all her strength and broke away from Mike. Though she loathed those three top dolls, Susan snatched them up. Break them—tear them—get rid of them! That was all she could think of.

Only, when she tried to snap their bodies, it was like trying to break a piece of iron. Burn them then! She looked around wildly. There was no fire on the big hearths of the downstairs fireplaces—but there might be matches, there was always the kitchen . . .

Dolls grasped tightly in both her hands, for she had a feeling that they might even now somehow get away from her, Susan burst through the door of her room. Down to the library where there was a fireplace and perhaps matches—or into the kitchen. She must do this—now! Then Tucky would be safe—safe as all the others had not been.

"Susan!" Mike caught at her arm. She did not even turn her head to look at him.

"Got to burn them!" she cried out as she pulled free and ran down the hall.

There was someone coming up the stairs—she was

164

only dimly aware that Great-Aunt Hendrika had appeared. But there was also a startled cry from behind. A moment later a small, compact body thudded so hard against her that she was unbalanced and slammed face down before she reached the head of the stairs.

Hands caught painfully at her hair, pulling, then beating on her shoulders.

"No! No! No!" Tucky's voice.

The dolls had been under her in a tight hold. To Susan it seemed that they were no longer flat. They were rounding, fighting against her. She gasped and tried to hold on. If they got away—then—she did not know what might happen but it would be something terrible. The fear that had been a part of her all this night was like a big black cloud—and she could not hold on much longer to those things turning and struggling under her.

"Susan—Tucker! Martha, come and help me!"

The pounding on her back had stopped. But Susan could not hold any longer. She could not keep them—burn them—they were too strong. She knew she was crying, and she was cold, so terribly cold, as if the things she held were bits of ice, able to send out waves of chill striking all the way through her.

Her hands ached, numb with cold, with the pain that came of trying to keep her fingers curved about the three bits of wood and ancient paper as they fought for freedom.

It was growing darker. The light in the hall dimmed. *They* drew strength from the dark. She—could—not—hold . . .

There was nothing in her hands. But at the top of

165

the stair now, as she tried to pull herself up, three figures crouched. Susan could sense what they felt, knew exactly what they knew. There was no way she could escape what was coming. It was as if she were being pulled into the middle of those three.

No! She was Susan—she was not Johanna—she was Susan! As she had tried to hold to the dolls, so she now held with all her strength to that. Susan—Susan—Susan . . .

There came a sharp snap, as if she had broken a tight piece of string. She was no longer being pulled into Johanna. Though she still could feel the fear of that other one who had been a doll without a face and now was something else—something that had no place in Susan's world at all.

Fear—something terrible going to happen. Susan could not stop it. But now she was an onlooker, not a part of it. Someone was coming up the stairs very fast, taking two steps at a time. The boy who was Carolus had moved a little away from the other two, stepping between them and whoever came. Though the hallway was dark in one way—still Susan could see clearly all three of those others. They grew brighter and more visible with every breath she drew.

Carolus had a gun—a strange-looking gun with a long barrel. It was so heavy that, even when he used both hands to raise it, it wobbled back and forth. And Susan knew that he was unable to hold it steady, though his need to use it struck through the clouds of fear to touch her.

There was a man at the top of the stairs. He wore a green coat—but below that breeches of leather with fringes along the sides. His head was bare and his hair was long and had been tied back with a piece of black ribbon. His face was very brown, the cheekbones standing out sharply as if he had been hungry for a long time. Straight across his face and on the bridge of his high beaked nose was a slash of yellow paint.

His mouth opened and his lips moved. Susan knew that he was saying something of importance to the three children he faced. All at once his hand shot out and caught the heavy gun away from Carolus, taking it very easily from the boy.

Whatever he was telling them seemed to make the feeling of fear ease a little, Johanna grasped Florian's hand, nodded, and then pulled at Carolus's sleeve, even though he held back, staring at the man as if he did not believe him.

Then—very faint and far away (as if it came through years of time—not just up from the lower part of the house) Susan heard a blast of noise. That made the man look behind him quickly, then catch Carolus by his shoulder, swing him around to push him down the stairs, beckoning the other two to follow.

Down they went—and Susan was going too, though she was so intent, so drawn by what she watched that she was not even aware of walking, of descending the stairs. They passed through the lower hall.

The sense of fear was mixed with a need for haste— something must be done and very quickly. Once more Susan heard, very distantly, screams and shouts. They came into the kitchen. She had a misty view of the great fireplace with a fire burning in it—of changes here. Still everything was so strange and shadowy she could not get a clear view of anything but the four figures she accompanied—the man with his green coat, turning his head now and then to show the painted slash across his face, to make sure that the three children were folloing him.

The great door to the cellarway was a little open. He pulled it back, snatching up from the floor a candle enclosed in a box that had holes in its sides so that light came through. Holding it in front of him, he started down the stairs.

Susan wanted nothing so much as to stay where she was, in that misty-cornered kitchen where the walls were half-hidden in a fog. Only the others drew her on. The lantern light gave very little help. She had a smaller fear beneath the greater one of tripping and falling to the stone floor underneath. But somehow she made it down. The lower hall with its doors opening into the storage rooms—it was no longer here—she could see that much even in so poor a light. Things like huge barrels were lined up against one wall, great chests of wood, other boxes. The man in the green coat turned to the right. He came to a rough wall of stone, showing no windows or any opening. Setting his lantern down on the top of a barrel, laying beside it the big gun he had taken from Carolus, he faced the wall, began to run his hands up and down over it. What he was hunting Susan could not guess.

The fear that had struck so sharply in the upper hallway was back. She was partly Johanna—a very small part—and the dark—what this man would do—made her stiff inside with terror. Something happened to the wall. There was an opening, dark and even more frightening, where moments earlier there had been just solid stone.

The man grabbed up the lantern and the pistol. Turning to Carolus he held out both to the boy who took them as if he did not want to, but knew that he must. It was Carolus who waved to his brother and sister, standing hand and hand, urging them on into the hole while he held high the lantern.

For a very long moment Johanna did not move. Susan was a part of her fear of the dark—of this place she did not know and that she hated to enter. Then she glanced down at Florian, and drawing the younger boy closer to her full skirt, she went on, Carolus following them, still holding high his lantern.

Once more the man in green faced the wall, placed his hands high against it on either side of the hole. For a second time Susan could not see just what had happened, she only was sure that the hole had closed. And once it closed, he was gone also. Dark—thick, black and horrible—held her, and she screamed, the very force of that cry rasping her sore throat painfully.

Dark—she was caught in the dark—forever and ever— and ever . . . !

"Mike! Tucky!" She found breath enough past the heavy weight of the dark pressing in upon her to call their names.

"Susan! Mike! Tucker!"

Who was that? At least she was not alone here!

"Please—please . . . !" Her voice began high in a near scream, dwindled to a whimper.

There was light flooding about Susan, dazing and dazzling her so that for a moment, she was blinded by it and had to blink and blink. She was back—in that room where they had found Tucky beating on the wall—the wall that had once had a door and was now sealed.

Susan felt so weak she feared she was going to fall, then Mike was there—standing right beside her. And—and there was Tucky, facing the wall.

"Miss Hendrika, you all right? What in the world's going on down here?" came Mrs. Kingsley's voice from a distance.

Susan turned her head a fraction. There was Great-Aunt Hendrika standing just within the storeroom door. Her hands were pressed against her cheeks, her face was very pale, her eyes were wide. Just like Tucky, she stared at the wall. And Susan realized that perhaps all of them had seen—might even have felt—what she herself had seen and felt.

"In there." Tucker pointed with one of his bandaged hands. "They have waited so long—right in there."

"All right, Tuck." Mike moved forward and caught his brother, drawing Tucker's small pajama-clad body close to him. Then, shedding his own robe, he wrapped it around Tucker. "We know now."

Though Tucky made no attempt to pull free of his brother, he continued to look to the wall another long moment before he turned his head up to Mike.

"They want out."

Mike nodded. "We'll get them, Tucky, as soon as we can, we'll get them."

Susan shook her head slowly. Even now she could not believe that she was not caught up in a nightmore —that she was not dreaming all this. The pressing-down fear was gone, leaving her feeling very queer and limp—as she had after she had had the flu last year.

"Children . . . " Great-Aunt Hendrika's voice had certainly lost all its commander-of-the-base power. She sounded like Susan felt—weak and shaky. "Children . . . " she began again.

But she could not find the right words. Mike drew Tucker back from that solid wall.

"You saw it, too," he said to her, not asking a question, just stating a fact.

Great-Aunt Hendrika made a queer sound. Then she spoke clearly again and with some of her old forcefulness. "I saw—yes, I saw. Come."

She swept forward and caught up Tucky. Carrying him, held tight against her, she sidled out of the storage-room sidewise, her attention still on that wall. Tucker did not fight her, instead he had relaxed in her arms, now rested his head against her shoulder. Susan stumbled after them, Mike catching up, his arm flung about his sister's shoulders, giving her warmth and support she had never wanted so much in her whole life before.

Mrs. Kingsley was halfway down the cellar stairs.

"What in—" She began a question. Then something in Great-Aunt Hendrika's face silenced her. Instead she turned and went up quickly, letting them past before she switched out the light, closed the door, setting the crossbar in place once more.

Great-Aunt Hendrika got as far as the rocking chair and dropped into it, Tucky still in her arms. He looked as if he were asleep, his eyes were closed, and he was breathing evenly.

171

"A hot drink . . . " Great-Aunt looked to Mrs. Kingsley. "I think we can all well do with that, Martha. This has been—Oh, I refuse to think about it now. I don't know what to believe—after tonight I simply do not know."

Mrs. Kingsley handed Mike the old crocheted afghan, which lay on one of the fireplace settles, and he wrapped it around him in place of the robe Tucky wore. Mrs. Kingsley put a kettle on the stove, set out mugs, then rummaged in the cupboard for a jar from which she measured what looked like tea into a big pot. She also got out the honey jar.

"Best mixture for nerves—honey—need that for shock." She might be talking to herself. "Drink this good and hot, then perhaps the whole lot of you won't come down with colds. I don't know what's been happening—but it seems mighty upsetting whatever." She paused a moment, as she went toward the kettle—which was beginning to make boiling noises, to look at the cellar door.

"To tell the truth—I never did fancy going down in that place. Never said it before but I do now. There's something mighty unhealthy down there. Never does to give into nerves and I never have, but—" She shrugged, took the tea kettle off the stove and poured the water into the waiting pot.

"Give it a good minute or two. Then you'll all drink it down!" There was a sergeant's emphasis in her voice. "I would like to know, though, how that young one got past me. One minute he was safe in his bed and I thought he'd gone off to sleep, the next I was looking at an empty bed. And when I went hunting him, all of you had gone—just as if you had disappeared into thin air. Like one of those old stories . . . "

Great-Aunt Hendrika straightened a little. Some color had returned to her face, and she looked more like herself.

"Stories? What have you heard, Martha?"

When Mrs. Kingsley did not answer at once, she spoke more sharply: "I want to know. Oh, you need not mind saying anything in front of the children—not after tonight. I think perhaps they know more than a great many who have lived under this roof in the past had even begun to guess."

Mrs. Kingsley produced a small strainer and poured the tea through it into the waiting mugs.

"You know yourself, Miss Hendrika, that there are some folks about as would not stay a night under this roof for a farm, as my father used to say. There's always been a cloud over this house (though I will admit that in the new wing one doesn't feel it) ever since that day of blood. I'm a sensible woman and have been all my days. Never took to imagining things even when I was as small as that tad you're holding now. But there are feelings sometimes—and I must be well shook out of myself to admit that much.

"It's always the children, though, it acted upon. Not those who are full grown. Not all children either. Maybe those affected the most had a drop more of the old blood somehow. You need only do a little thinking back yourself, Miss Hendrika. I remember when Grover died and your Cousin Hester vowed she'd never set foot under this roof again. He was found down in the cellar, and he went into a real high fever. Said

173

some strange things then. Finally he got away from that nurse they brought from the city and fell—down those cellar steps. He was so weak they judged he missed a step and just tumbled.

"There were others, too—"

"Jethro and Emily, Richard and Tod, and James . . ." Susan said slowly. Once more, like a shadow quickly gone, she felt a touch of fear chill within her.

Now Mrs. Kingsley swung around, the tea dripping from the strainer into the sink, to stare at the girl.

"Where—where did you hear tell of them?" she asked.

"They were in the Bible. And they are the dolls, too. Jethro and Emily died in 1851, and Richard and Tod in 1880, and James—he was after. But Betsy and the two Orrins and Hester—they didn't die—until much later. Mike looked it up. Only all of them are the dolls— all of them! Just like Johanna, and Carolus and Florian—who were the first ones—the real ones!" Why they were any more real than the others Susan could not have explained, she was only sure that they were.

"The dolls," Great-Aunt Hendrika said. "Yes, the dolls. But why didn't Hester destroy them when she hated the family custom so? She always swore that she would. I remember she would not even look at them when Aunt Bess made them for Christmas and gave them to her—the set with her own self among them, added to the old ones. And—" She shook her head. "I am not going to make any guesses, I can't. This goes beyond guessing, and I want to talk to someone who can understand.

"Tucker"—her voice was a little more brisk—"do

174

you think you can drink a little of this?"

She had braced him up and was holding the mug
Mrs. Kingsley had given her to his lips. His eyes opened
slowly and he obediently accepted a sip. Susan held
another mug between her hands and so did Mike. The
darkish liquid tasted a little like peppermint and was
sweet. As it went down Susan's throat, she began to
feel warm inside and oddly, as if something very
heavy she had been carrying for a long time had been
taken away from her, leaving her free and very sleepy.
If she could just get to bed, Susan thought, she was
going to sleep and sleep and sleep—and never dream
again.

Chapter

12

THERE WERE FLARING LIGHTS ON ALL over the house and for that Susan was very glad. She came back up those stairs, down which Johanna, Carolus, Florian, and the painted man had gone, to stumble into her own room where more lights banished all shadows. Even so, she made a detour so that she could not even look sidewise into the misty mirror. On the bed was the box she had emptied so hastily—and the two piles of dolls.

There also lay the three which she had taken up, wanting to burn—to destroy them. There were faces on them now. She could see them. But, though she put out her hand very slowly to touch them, there was nothing frightening about them now. All that fear was gone. These were only paper—old paper cut into patterns, pasted and glued together. They were just dolls. Swiftly she repacked them layer by layer in the box, pressed the lid tightly down. Then rummaging in her school case she found a roll of tape and sealed the box around and around—finally pushing it into the bottom of the big wardrobe.

Susan snapped the light switch and made for bed, half throwing herself beneath the covers, pulling them tightly up around her shoulders, for she was shivering, but the cold was no longer inside her. She thumped her head determinedly back on her pillow and closed her eyes. Though in her was still a small touch of fear. Was she going to dream—about *them?*

"Sue! Sue!"

At first that call sounded faint and far away. Then came a pounding—a pounding on a wall that would not open again? Susan's eyes snapped open as a sharp thrust of fear ran through her. The room was not dark. Bright sun shone across the bed, touched the walls. Also she felt— Susan shook her head. She could not have explained just how she felt—just that for the first time since she had come into this room it was only that—a plain room—with strange old furniture—but still a place in which people—just ordinary people like Mike, and Tucky, Mother and Dad, and Susan—had lived and been happy and sometimes sad. There were no shadows now in the corners. They no longer had the right to be there!

"Sue!" Again that pounding. That was certainly Mike's voice from the hallway. She slid swiftly out of bed. It must be late—there was so much sun in the room. And she felt hungry, as if the time for breakfast was well past.

"I'm here." She opened the door. Her brother was

dressed and frowning a little.

"You sure can sleep! The G.-A. sent me up to see what was the matter."

"What time is it?"

Mike did not even look at his watch. From below stairs, carrying all the way up to them, came the bong of the big hall clock. Ten strokes! Susan was more than a little surprised. Ten? She had slept that late?

"Tucky?"

"Eating up half the muffins," Mike reported. "If you want any you had better get a move on. Mrs. Kingsley's pretty flustered this morning and we're having a mixed-up lot of things to eat."

"Great-Aunt Hendrika?" Susan was more than a little surprised at Tucker's quick recovery. Though he did have a habit of bouncing back from colds, and he had been the first one to get through the chicken pox they had all had at one time. Once he made up his mind that he was well Tucky just was.

"She made some phone calls—and then she went out," Mike reported. "I think she's gone now to see Mr. Reevers down at the church. That Dr. Ferguson, she called him first, asked him to come back."

"I'll hurry," Susan promised as Mike went on to his room, coming back, as she passed him in the hall on the way to the bathroom, with the big brown diary book under his arm.

Dressing was a sketchy business, which Susan did in a hurry. She didn't use her hairbrush, or look in the mirror. Not because she was afraid of that misty old glass any longer, but because she was hungry, and from what Mike had said there was something unusual

178

awaiting them all.

Mrs. Kingsley was at the sink, washing the plates and cups with such clatter that Susan wondered whether most of them would come out lacking a handle or chipped along the edge.

"Serve yourself," she said as Susan came to the table. Tucker sat on the kitchen stool, running his tongue upward to lick off the smear of mingled jam and milk on his upper lip. Susan stared. Last night might never have been, except for the now somewhat grimy looking bandages around her brother's hands.

She scraped the last of the oatmeal out of the pot on the stove into a bowl, and then helpfully carried the pot to the waiting-to-be-washed pile. There was brown sugar in its own dish, and this she sifted over her cereal, watching Tucker. He met her eyes with an odd sidewise glance of his own, as if he did not want to talk, and crammed another muffin into his mouth.

Susan ate slowly, but somehow she was no longer so hungry. Inside, she felt the old familiar tightness growing in her stomach. Up above in her bedroom, she had felt free and light. Down here—Susan made herself look deliberately across the width of the table to the barred cellar door—down here something else was going to happen!

She stopped eating, no longer hungry. It even made her queasy to see Tucker munching away. In fact, it made her uneasy to watch Tucker at all. It was as if he knew something that was not only exciting but dreadfully frightening, and that he thought about it all the time. Sooner or later he was going to tell Susan what she did not want in the least to hear.

"That all you going to eat, child?" Mrs. Kingsley saw Susan folding up her napkin.

"I—I don't feel very hungry. Just don't want any more, thank you."

Mrs. Kingsley shook her head. "All right then, run along with you. Miss Hendrika has some errands. She won't be back for a while."

Run where—to the library? What about Tucker? He had finished the last of the muffins with what Susan considered unsightly gorging, but had made no move to get down from his stool perch and go to wash as he had always been sternly ordered to do. It would seem that Mrs. Kingsley expected him to stay where he was. Slowly Susan cleaned up after herself and then went down the hall to the library.

Mike was there, on the window seat where Tucky had sat earlier, the diary of Jacobus Kuydall spread open on one knee. He was squinting down at the dim writing on one page when Susan marched over to him.

"Mike—what is going to happen?" She pressed one hand hard to settle her unhappy stomach. She was not horribly afraid as she had been last night, but there was still the knowledge that ahead of them lay trouble of some sort. "Tucky doesn't seem sick this morning."

"No." Mike's answer was a putting-off one, but Susan refused to allow that to matter.

"Did Great-Aunt Hendrika call Mother and Dad?"

"I don't think so. She had other things to think about, I guess." Mike sounded angry.

"Should we, if she did forget?" Susan persisted.

"Later—maybe . . . " He suddenly turned the book around so that Susan could see for herself a very much

180

faded colored picture that took up one whole page.

"That's—that's Great-Aunt Hendrika—and—and ... " Susan was startled.

The woman in the picture stood very stiffly, wearing a strange brown dress that was fringed and had a patterning of beads on the shoulders and around the neck. Strings of what looked to be the teeth or claws of animals formed two necklaces and her hair was in two long braids framing her strong-featured face. In her hand she held against her body, as if it were a shield, a painted mask with the mouth drawn down to one side, the eyes very large and outlined heavily with black. Across the nose of the carved face ran a broad band of yellow like the one Susan had seen on the face of the green-coated man. Only he had been real—no mask or picture.

Beside the woman was a man. The upper part of his body was bare except for a necklace of claws, very long claws, and on his chest was painted a queer-looking bird, its wings outstretched. The bird had been painted in red and blue, and there were two small blue stripes on the man's chin, and a yellow line starting between his eyes and running up his hairline.

His head was very strange, shaved bare over his ears up to near the top of his skull. There an upstanding spiky growth of hair ran from front to back. On his legs he wore tightly fitting, fringed breeches, and there were moccasins on his feet. One of his hands had been drawn as if reaching out for the mask the woman held. Susan had an idea that she did not intend to give it to him.

"Who are they?"

181

"This one"—Mike pointed a finger at the woman—"is someone called Strong Woman. She—well, I suppose maybe you'd call her a witch. Anyway, they all believed she could give you good luck or bad, whichever she thought you deserved. And this—I think it might just be Jacobus, only it doesn't say so . . . " He indicated the man. "He wanted a lot of power and he thought he might get it through her. Only she did not favor him much. This tells about a ceremony of some sort, but ends by saying that fortune was not favorable."

"If he had more hair and a green coat . . . " Susan ventured.

"Yes—Jacobus, the renegade." Mike closed the book. "This"—he held up the old volume—"doesn't go far enough. It ends right after the big meeting of the Six Nations where Sir William Johnson tried to keep the tribes neutral."

Susan was remembering what Mike had told Tucker. "He was the one who died."

Mike nodded. "He died. Then others won out and the Nations joined the British. That was the start of it all."

"Jacobus . . . " Susan moved farther into the sun patch by the window. Somehow she wanted it around her now. "*Was* it Jacobus?" she asked in a low voice. "That man we saw?"

Mike dropped the book on the desk with a distinct bang.

"Was it anything?" he demanded. "People don't see things that happened two hunderd years ago—"

"How do you know?" Susan demanded. "How do you know what any of us could see or not see? You and Dad—don't you remember how you talked that time about how there was a lot of our brains we didn't use at all—that no one could understand why or what that part was even intended to do? So there are people who *can* do things that are strange and queer, and frightening. Why, even in the space program, they were thinking of trying to see if people were telepathic and could send messages that way. I heard Dad talking about it with Dr. Stangley and Colonel Pitts right at our own table back home.

"And Tucky—you know that Tucky tested clear off some of those old charts that Dr. Ramish had and how excited the doctor was about that. Maybe Tucky is one of those who has a chance to use part of his closed-off mind—maybe it was Tucky's coming here that started it all for us." She was guessing, but it seemed to her that there was something true about this guessing.

Mike ran his hand along the edge of the desk, almost as if he were wiping the feel of the book from it. Then he turned around, his back to her, his shoulders hunched a little. Susan felt the excitement in her growing—and this time it did not make her feel sick.

"Something important is going to happen." She spoke her main thought out loud.

Mike stood very still, his hand stopping in mid-sweep. Then he turned to face her again.

"Yes." He answered as if he did not want to say the word at all but had to.

"Did Great Aunt say—" Susan began.

"She didn't say anything to me. And she closed the door to the hall when she phoned from downstairs. We'll just have to wait."

How long, Susan wondered to herself. There was a queer shut-in expression on Mike's face. There were always times, though not too many of them, when he would not talk about things. There was no use her prodding and poking to find out what or why.

Susan went over to the bookshelf and ran her fingers along the backs of the books. The ones on the first shelf—Emily had maybe read those—or Jethro. Then came those that Richard and Tod had held. And James's . . . They had all been real once—not just names, and paper dolls, but real people like Mike, and her, and Tucker. Just as the others had been real— Johanna, Carolus, Florian. There were no books here with those names written in them—maybe there were no books for children way back in those days. She fingered a book on the second shelf, pulled it out and marched over to the window seat with it in hand.

Granny's Wonderful Chair. Susan had refused to look for the name of an owner in the front. Now she began doggedly to read. It was the only way she could think of to try and forget or subdue her feelings of something ahead—something that was—no, she was through being frightened! She would not be frightened!

They had lunch promptly at twelve. Tucker had seemingly spent the morning in the kitchen. When they were called by Mrs. Kingsley, he was, of all things, seated in the rocking chair, while squeezed in beside him was Josiah who opened his eyes lazily as Mike and Susan entered. Tucker had one hand deep in the thick fur of the cat's back and was in the midst of a story about last Halloween when Jimmy Smithers back home had carved out a real pumpkin and put a black kitten inside until his mother caught him at it. It was as if the Tucker they had known since they came to the Kuydall house had never existed at all.

"Gingerbread!" he greeted his sister and brother. "And I got the lickin' of the bowl. Uhmmm!"

In spite of her unease Susan managed a better lunch, but they were still at the table when they heard a car come into the side yard. A moment or two later Great-Aunt Hendrika came through the back door, bringing with her not only Mr. but Mrs. Reevers.

"Any calls?" she aked abruptly before they were fairly inside.

"He'll be here at two, Miss Hendrika, called his friend long distance, and those two will drive up—him and some other man. Didn't catch the name of that one. Jim went over to the Evers' to get help—so that's all arranged for. I got things ready in the dining room, you folks just go on in. Eloise"—her mouth turned down at the corners in marked disapproval—"she has taken a headache—or so she says."

Susan watched Great-Aunt Hendrika and the Reevers go on down the hall. The fact that they were not sharing any lunch with the Whelans must mean that they were talking over something. She knew the signs. Mrs. Reevers, however, did stop for a moment beside Tucker's chair and ask him how he felt, to be answered by a wide grin and some indistinct words impolitely uttered around a full mouthful of gingerbread.

At two there were indeed more arrivals. The library had been off limits, the Whelans judged, when the Reevers and Great-Aunt Hendrika had withdrawn there after lunch and closed the door. So they had gone outside into the crisp air and wandered around, Tucker kicking up the drifts of leaves the wind was bringing down. Jim was not working at the compost pile. Instead he had brought out two heavy bars of metal, a couple of spades, and a big pickaxe, setting them up against the side of what had once been the barn. There was another man standing there watching, but when the Whelans would have joined them, Jim told them, in a not-to-be-contradicted voice, to run along.

Dr. Ferguson came, with him two other men who went directly to the front door of the house. It was only minutes later when Mrs. Kingsley opened the back door and waved to the children, beckoning them in.

The library seemed full of people when the three went in to join Great-Aunt Hendrika, who was sitting behind the desk, with Dr. Ferguson on one side and Mr. Reevers on the other.

"Susan, will you go and get the dolls?" Great-Aunt Hendrika's voice was calm and as forceful as ever. Susan found it easy to obey, leaving to fetch the taped-up box she had hidden.

When she returned, they were not looking toward the door as if they expected her, rather they were all watching Tucker and he was talking.

"They waited—and waited . . . " He held up both bandaged hands balled into fists as if he were again pounding on the wall. " 'Cause they were hiding when the bad men were in the house. Just like they were told—"

"And who told them, Tucker?" asked the strange man Dr. Ferguson had brought along (one of them—

186

the other—seemed to have disappeared. At least he was not in the room now).

"The man—the man who showed them the place to wait." Tucker shook his head. "He—he was a bad one, but he thought they would be safe there."

"How do you know that?" The same quiet voice asked the question as Susan same forward and laid the box of dolls on the desk top.

"I just know." There was a shade of stubbornness on Tucker's face. "They believed him. But he never came—he promised but he never came!" He shook his head violently from side to side.

Dr. Ferguson spoke then to Great-Aunt Hendrika. "Was there any family tradition of any such a place? I have heard of hiding holes in case of attack."

"None in our traditions or records," she repeated firmly. "Of course, Jacobus was here when his father died, and his brother was not. There was not much sympathy between the father, old Jacobus, and Hendrik at the time, because Hendrik was serving with Washington's army in the East. Such a secret might have been shared only with the son the father favored."

Tucker sat swinging his feet, watching the people on the other side of the desk with bright interest. Maybe he was going to add some " 'maginings" now, but he did not say anything.

It was to Susan that the man who asked the questions now turned.

"These are the dolls?" He put out his hand toward the box she pushed closer with a good shove. Let him open it up. Even though she did not fear them any more, somehow she did not want to handle them again.

187

He peeled off the tape she had used and then brought them out, arranging them on the top of the desk, discarding their clothing but looking closely at each doll—turning it over to read the name on the back, bringing out a small magnifying glass to study the faces.

"Undoubtedly these must have been painted from life—and quite skillfully," he said of Jethro, Emily, and the first Orrin, "while these are from photographs. They were intended to resemble real children. Who made them?"

For a second or two Susan thought that Great-Aunt Hendrika was not going to answer, then she did in a low voice.

"By tradition, Jethro, Emily and Orrin were by their mother. She had some talent as a painter of miniatures, it is said. They were made in imitation of the first three Kimbles. The others—" She shook her head. "I do not honestly know—except it had become a family tradition somehow. Those, however—" She indicated the three of wood and skin. "There is a story about them, which is another family tradition. Mistress Hughes is said to have made them."

"Ah—" That came from Dr. Ferguson, almost like a sigh. He reached down to take from a briefcase beside his chair a bundle of printed sheets held together in a clear plastic sack. "Mistress Hughes! Also known as Strong Woman—the famous Oneida witch!"

Great-Aunt's head came up sharply. "She was no more a witch than I am. A healer, yes. She was with Betje Kuydall when the raid started, but it was her house that was attacked first, although she was not there, any more than Betje was here. They were both with a woman having a difficult birth. Margaret Hughes was part Oneida, yes, and they believed she had powers. The Indians did not touch her. But the renegades killed her son and her daughter. Some said that Jacobus ordered it because she had crossed him in some way, even though she was close kin through his mother. Something to do with the power he always craved and wanted to seize here.

"Yes, the story of the curse started then. Margaret Hughes turned against all the Kuydalls. After the raid she went away—nor was she heard of again, though Hendrik searched for her as well as for his children. It is all in that—" She waved one hand to the packet of loose pages Dr. Ferguson held.

Susan glanced down at the three first dolls. Yes, even as had been true this morning, the faces were now plain. At least *she* could see them and they were the same faces the shadowy people had worn.

Having arranged the dolls to his liking, the man gazed once more at Susan.

"Tell me," he said, "what happened last night?"

She twisted her hands in the belt that held up her jeans. No, she did not want to remember—even though it was all past now. Only something was making her. Just as last night something had made her follow those four, who had been shadows and then became people, down the stairs and through the house.

Taking a deep breath, Susan began—with her dream and the hands reaching out to her—with Tucker's sleepwalking and their visit to the cellar—and finally with the need to destroy the dolls and how that had taken her into the hall. So, as she talked, she watched

189

the man in green come up the stairs again. Once she had started, she could not have stopped talking even if she had been allowed to. Her words came faster and faster, as if she were seeing it all over again. Except that the fear was now dulled and she could push it aside. When she finished, the man turned to Mike.

From Mike came another version of the same adventure. Only Mike added more details, how he had pulled Tucker off his sister when she had taken the dolls to destroy them and had fallen in the hall, and of his own sight of the four they followed, three of whom had vanished into the wall slit.

"Miss Kuydall—" Now the man with the quiet, almost gentle voice spoke to their great aunt.

"Dr. Winston, I can only repeat what I have said earlier. I have never believed in such things. Oh, I have read many accounts of so-called haunted houses, everyone does at one time or another, I am sure. I have always slept in the portion of the house that was added about 1840, and I have never seen or heard of anything out of the ordinary—until last night. My cousin Hester—she hated this house, and it is true that one of her brothers, as a young boy, died here. He had been ill and was sent here to convalesce. Then her son Grover . . . he had a bad case of the flu and was found dead at the bottom of the cellar stairs—supposed to have wandered in his fever. Hester came to believe firmly in what is termed the 'curse.'

"But what my great niece and nephew—and Tucker—have told you, though Tucker's reactions were the strongest, is essentially true for last night. I, too, saw exactly what they did. I—what can I believe

190

now—?" She turned her head a little and looked to Mr. Reevers. "Did we actually witness something that happened? Or was it a mass hallucination of some type? If so, what induced it among the four of us? Mrs. Kingsley saw nothing. Also she was oddly unaware that Tucker had even left his bed until we were all downstairs. Was it because we were Kuydalls by blood that only we were so affected?"

"There is no answer I can give you," Mr. Reevers said slowly. "There are many theories—yes . . . Perhaps Dr. Winston can offer one or two—"

"Many theories indeed. One is that a deeply emotional happening makes a print of itself, just as a camera takes a picture, upon the area in which that action occurred. People who are sensitive to the emotion can pick up sights, sounds, even a reinactment of the action if the conditions are right.

"Also it is well known that children attract certain forces we do not understand, for all our probing. The poltergeist phenomenon is often associated with some young person of the disturbed household. From past events here"—he glanced down once more at the paper dolls—"it would appear that children inheriting the Kuydall blood—some of them—were sensitive to a strange influence. You have said that in two cases this came after the child had been seriously ill. Many times psychic powers are awakened by illness. I can give you no real answer. Though I do believe that you saw—all of you"—he stared the longest at Tucker—"did see exactly what you have reported. And that it has a meaning—which should be investigated."

Chapter

13

THE THIRD MAN, THE STRANGER WHO
had driven in with Dr. Ferguson,
had come in while Dr. Winston was speaking. Great-
Aunt Hendrika spoke directly to him in her old "commander" voice.

"Well, Mr. Standish?"

"There is no outward sign of any kind," he returned.
"However, I would say that the wall there is unusually
thick, even though our measurements have had to be
mostly by guess. Without any clues the only answer
is to try and take out some of the stones—at the right
place. But to discover that—"

Tucker slid off his chair and went directly to the
stranger.

"You want to let them out! I'll show you—I know!"
The words seemed to explode out of him. He turned
and made for the door of the library, passing Susan

and Mike before they could grab him. All the others were startled for a moment, simply watching him go. But Susan, though she had herself not the slightest wish to return to that bad-smelling place underground, hurried after him. Mike was only a step or two behind. And she thought, from the sounds she heard, that all the others were following.

They passed through the kitchen, where there was no sign of Mrs. Kingsley. Just as they had been before, the two big cats were seated in front of the barred cellar door, staring at it as if the silent demand they seemed to be making would at last open it.

Tucker reached up to jerk at the bar. It moved but he did not have strength enough to lift it. Mike pushed his brother aside to slide it out, dropping it to the floor with a thud. Susan pressed the back of her hand against her mouth. She was not going to be sick. She could not be—not now.

The door opened and Mike caught Tucker, holding him by a handful of T-shirt between his shoulders, until he found the light switch. But the two cats had not waited for that. They vanished down the stairs together, so quickly Susan hardly saw their disappearing tail tips.

With the light on, and the steps clear before them, Mike loosed his hold on Tucker. He had to, for the smaller boy had swung halfway round to pound his brother's midsection with his bandaged hands. Tucker's face was bright red. He was plainly building up a burst of real temper and a steep stairs was no place for any struggle.

As the cats had done, Tucker shot down the stairs so

193

fast Susan was afraid he would lose his footing and fall. She had to keep one hand on the rail beside her because she once more felt that queer floating that had hit her last night. Mike was a little ahead as they both saw Tucker head straight for the storeroom where they had found him earlier.

He was back at the wall when they squeezed through the door together. On either side of him sat one of the cats, watching the wall with the same eager attention with which they had watched the closed door above. Then the others came in—Great-Aunt Hendrika, the Reevers, Dr. Ferguson, Dr. Winston, and Mr. Standish, who seemed to know about walls. There were two others following him, Jim and another man in workclothes.

Tucker paid no attention to the people crowding into the room behind him. He had gone very close to the wall, standing on tiptoe, stretching his hands well over his head. Then he moved slowly along from right to left, though as far as Susan could see he did not touch any of the rough stones. He stopped short, to pat the wall.

"Here! Right here!" His voice was high and excited, though he did not turn to face any of those behind him in the storeroom.

"The outer wall." That was Great-Aunt Hendrika. "But there is nothing there. You can see—nothing!"

Susan thought she sounded as if she wanted to believe that was true, even though, deep inside her, she knew that it was not.

"Let me see, son." Mr. Standish moved quickly up beside Tucker, pushing past Susan and Mike. Josiah snarled and spat at him, but grudgingly moved aside. Though there was a light hanging from a cord in the ceiling, Mr. Standish held a big camper's torch and now centered its full beam on the old stones.

Flakes of old whitewash showed here and there, but mostly the gray of the stone was dark and damp looking. He moved very close, Tucker standing aside as if willing to yield place to him. He pushed a fingertip here and there, as if picking at the mortar between the old stones.

"No evidence that I can see . . . " he began.

Tucker uttered a yell of real anger, such as Susan and Mike had heard only too many times before in their lives. He shoved against the man's leg and strained up on his toes to pound one fist against the stone, crying out in pain at it.

"In there!" he nearly screamed and ended by kicking at the stones.

"All right, all right." Mr. Standish kept the torch on the wall. "Don't get yourself so heated up about it, son." He looked at the others. "It is up to you, Miss Kuydall. Do we try it?"

Great-Aunt Hendrika's face, in the dimmer light of the storeroom, looked queer. Her eyes, behind the lenses of her glasses, seemed as large as they did last night and her lips were very tight together. Susan watched her. Did Great-Aunt Hendrika feel a little as Susan did now—afraid and sick? Then those tight lips moved.

"It must be done." Great-Aunt Hendrika's voice was low and hoarse. She also made a small gesture with her hand.

They all crowded back against the rough wooden walls, pushing for room among the piles of baskets and crates. Even Tucker and the cats moved aside to give more space to Jim and the other man who were carrying a pick and a big iron bar.

However, it was Mr. Standish who took a piece of chalk from his pocket and, after a moment of studying the wall, marked a narrow strip up and down between certain stones. He stood a little to one side, as Jim brought the pickaxe down.

They might have expected to have a long hard job. At least they had come prepared for that. But at the second blow, a grating noise echoed through the room. Jim and his coworker jumped back to escape the fall of a whole section of stones. Though they appeared separate, they had all been fastened to a piece of wood that broke apart as it hit the cellar floor.

Susan gave a small gasp and reached out. She was glad to meet Mike's hand, even if he grabbed her fingers so tightly it was painful. A dank, evil smell, far worse than the one that had always been in the cellar, came from the hole beyond. Jim and his helper moved to one side as Mr. Standish stepped forward to flash the torch beyond.

Susan's mouth felt dry and with the churning in her stomach . . . No, she would not throw up, she was determined about that. Mr. Standish stooped a little, swinging the light downward. Then he backed out. He turned around and his face looked nearly as odd as Great-Aunt Hendrika's had earlier.

It was Dr. Ferguson who spoke first:

"Is there anything there, Standish?"

"Yes, there is."

"Oh . . . !" The broken cry came from Great-Aunt Hendrika. Susan saw Mrs. Reevers catch her aunt's hand and hold it comfortingly between both of hers. But it was Mr. Reevers who moved forward to speak with authority.

"Please, Miss Kuydall—you—Marjory—the children —must go. We shall do everything that is necessary here. There is no reason—"

"So long, so very long . . . " Great-Aunt Hendrika's voice was hardly above a whisper. "Right here and so long . . . "

Mrs. Reevers had her arm around Great-Aunt Hendrika's shoulders. Great-Aunt Hendrika's mouth puckered up. She looked really ill. Susan edged away from the hole and was glad that Mike continued to hold her hand. It was Tucker who really surprised them.

He paid no attention to the hole in the wall, but came directly to stand before Great-Aunt Hendrika, looking up at her soberly.

"*They* are gone. They waited—but they don't have to wait any more. They've gone—truly. And—and—they only wanted to be free, to go."

She looked down into Tucker's earnest face turned up to hers. Then she gently loosened Mrs. Reevers' hold and stooped to catch Tucker up in a tight embrace. He did not try to free himself as he ordinarily would. Instead, he was smiling.

"It's all right, they've gone now," he repeated.

"Yes." She turned, Mrs. Reevers behind her and, still carrying Tucker, went out of the storeroom, Susan and

197

Mike behind. Whatever lay beyond that wall hole no longer mattered. What had been there—even if it was, as Dr. Weston said, only the remains of a terrible fear—that was gone, too.

They were gathered once more in the library, Tucker still sitting on Great-Aunt Hendrika's lap, but none of them talking very much, when Dr. Ferguson and Mr. Reevers returned. The men hesitated, as if they did not know just how to say what they wanted to.

"We'll bury them by the monument—and with a service," Great-Aunt Hendrika said. Though she still held Tucker gently, much of her old command had returned.

Mr. Reevers nodded. "Of course," he echoed her. "But there is something else you should know. Those children were not alone. I think that perhaps the true story is quite different from the evil one that has always been accepted. Perhaps there was a special need to let everyone know that."

Dr. Ferguson took up the story now. "There was another door now rotted through, beyond that inner space. It gave on a passageway that had collapsed. Between the door and that fall of earth was—well, I think it could only have been Jacobus. And he had been coming in from the other side—to set the children free. There were indications that he had been badly wounded. Perhaps he used his last strength to try and reach the children, just as he had hidden them from the raiders. He was not—"

"Perhaps," Great-Aunt Hendrika said slowly, "he was mad when he planned the raid and sanity returned to him too late. What must have been his burden then!"

"At least," Mr. Reevers said slowly, "they are all at peace now. Even if we do not know the full story and never will, the truth seems plain. We can guess—or hope—many things. But I do honestly believe that what we are about to do now will bring the old fear and horror to an end. There is too much evil in this unfortunate world. To be able to lay some shadows that linger is, in a way, a small reaching from the dark to the light. They shall be at peace, which is our promised heritage."

Susan did not know why she did it, but she went swiftly to the desk top where the dolls Dr. Weston had been examining were lying. With care she repacked them just as they had once lain in the box that had fallen apart, Johanna, Carolus, and Florian first—then all the others in the proper order. She set the lid firmly on the box befoe she went to Mr. Reevers, who was by the door, talking in a low voice to Dr. Ferguson.

"Please," she dared to interrupt and they both looked at her. "Please, bury these, too. They were a part of it. Let them be—" She thought of what he had just said—"let them all be at peace—Jethro and Emily, and the rest—all the rest!"

He did not seem to think that she was foolish, or that the dolls had no importance. He took the box from her very gently.

"Yes, I believe you are right, Susan. It all needs to be set to rest now. This house has all shadows, large and small, lifted from it. These shall indeed be at peace also."

It had been a long day and a queer one, Susan thought

that night. She knew that there were still some plans in which she and Mike and Tucker would also play a part. Because, after all, they had been drawn into it from the beginning. There would be a new grave in the cemetery—right by the monument—one that would contain three who had been together—waiting and waiting for so very long.

There would be a second unmarked grave, too, with old troubles and hatred forgotten, on the other side of that standing stone, because a man who had planned a great act of evil had, in the end, tried to save those he believed he hated.

There would be in that single grave a white box. Susan turned her head on her pillow and saw that moonlight touched the sampler, so faded it could hardly be read. Jethro and Emily, Richard and Tod, James—and perhaps Grover. They had all tried—and it had not been their fault that they had not succeeded. Tucker was different. Perhaps he was the only one whom those who waited could reach. And they had had to wait so long for him!

Maybe their counting of time was different. Susan gave a little sigh—she hoped it was different. Yes, she hoped that, to them, the wait had not seemed so long.

There was a thump on her bed which startled her, and then she felt paws kneading the hand she had half stretched out toward the moonlit wall. Erasmus crouched there, purring so loudly that she could hear him. Then he turned around and settled down, his head pillowed on her hand, and little by little the purring faded away.

Susan's eyes closed. The shadows were finally gone

and they would never be back. It was all finished and finished right—just as any story should be, any good story. The Kuydall house was queer and different, but it could be a real home. Susan wondered sleepily why she had thought of that. Then she was truly asleep and there were no dreams at all waiting for her now.